TRUSTING CHANCE

Carol Schaffer

Carrie

I woke up to the same alarm, same song, and the same routine. I set up, grab some clothes, take a shower, and relax at the kitchen table with a large cup of coffee in my hands. I can hear the clock ticking, as I continually tell myself its time to go to work.

I'm a grown woman living on my own who is divorced, and my daughter is grown with her own family in another state. My name is Carrie, and I'm sick of my boring life.

I am officially on vacation when I clock out of work later today. I've saved my money all year to be able to go somewhere. The problem is that I have no destination in mind. I usually plan everything to avoid rushing, but I always end my vacation time just as bored as when I left. This time I said fuck it all, let the wheels on my truck take me wherever they will. I need to have a little fun, and fun shouldn't be planned.

I walk into work, and see my best friend, slash coworker walking toward me at a fast pace.

"I'm so fucking jealous." Justine's eyes lite up with excitement for me.

"Come with me." I just stare at her. I've been badgering her for two weeks to come along on my journey.

"What, and leave all this?" Her hands twirl around the warehouse in her usual flare of drama.

"Be at my house by six o'clock tonight with a bag. Two weeks of freedom from our boring everyday life."

"You're crazy." She turns, and pours us both a coffee.

"Six o'clock." I take my coffee, and my clipboard to begin another day of boring counts, and hard labor.

After hours of checking inventory, its now time to use my muscles, and start loading the trucks.I work in a warehouse where we pack, and ship merchandise to stores all over the world.

My real passion in life is to write. The problem with writing is that it doesn't pay the bills, but I love it too much to ever stop.

"Lunch!" Justine hollers after the buzzer goes off.

"What did you bring today?" I stare, as she reaches into her cooler.

She always brings something from home that she cooked the night before. Justine has a house full of family. They are all grown, but still all live at home. Some days I envy her for not being lonely, but other days I don't know how she stands the chaos.

"Lasagna, garlic bread, salad, and cheesecake." She pulls bowl after bowl out.

"How in the hell do you stay so skinny?" I shake my head, as she begins to shovel it in.

"Dig in." She mumbles over a mouth full.

"Mmmm damn, I love your cooking." Conversation is almost non existent until I shove my bowl away.

"Cheesecake?" She belches.

"Save me a piece for later, I'm stuffed." I laugh, as she digs in with gusto.

I sit quietly wondering about my life.

"Carrie?.... Hey, Carrie.... Earth to Carrie!"

I pull myself back to the present. "Sorry, what?" I ask confused.

"You were a mile away. What is going on with you lately?" She squeezes my hand.

"I need a life." I whisper softly, as I stare back out across the eating area outside.

"You need to get laid, get drunk, and just let loose."

"So do you." I smile.

"I get laid plenty, but as for getting drunk, I could use a drink,"

"Your husband chasing you around the house again?" She shakes her head at me.

"Damn fool thinks we're still young."

"Hey, you're only as old as you feel."

"Then I feel ancient." She shrugs.

"Come with me." I grab her hand in mine, pleading.

"My house would fall apart without me."

"Do you want to go?"

"Yes, I would love to go, but Greg needs me." She laughs, as the buzzer sounds that lunch is over.

"Okay." I gather our trash feeling disappointed.

I spend the next five hours busting my ass off to get finished on time with all my jobs ,so I can go home.

I walk into my little apartment, and drop my bag. My clothes fall off in a trail behind me on my way to the shower.

I'm packed, and look around one more time to see if I have forgotten anything. I pack my truck tight, and I'm ready to roll to get this vacation started.

"Wait!"

I turn to Justine flying into my driveway. "No way!" I smile, just knowing why she is here.

"Greg said 'Why the hell not, you do for everyone, now dammit do something for yourself." She flings her suitcase in the back of my truck.

"Damn, I love that man!" I squeal, as I hug her.

"Yeah, he is pretty wonderful."

We jump up and down like school girls before we get in the truck.

"Road trip music!" I slide in Highway to Hell by AC/DC to get this trip started. I reach into my purse and pull a die with N S E W on it. I roll it on the dash and a W comes up. "West it is."

We drive for hours enjoying the country side, and the peacefulness of no work, or worries. I look over, and Justine is sleeping. I'm so happy that my best friend was able to share this trip with me. I needed to get out of my everyday rut. I feel like I'm stuck in a pattern with no changes ahead unless I make myself step outside of my comfort zone, and actually do something.

I was married too for a long time to a man who controlled my life, and I let myself become someone I didn't like. I've been divorced for quite a few years now, and my life is my own. I'm happy with me, but now I need to trust myself to just let go and enjoy.

It's been about eight hours driving, and I need to rest, so I find a hotel.

"Where are we?" Justine stretches awake when I shut the truck off.

"Somewhere in Mississippi. This is the first hotel I saw, and that's good enough for me." I get us a room with two beds, and we hit the sheets.

I'm dreaming about something relaxing when a loud banging jars me awake. I look at the clock that reads four thirty in the morning. I'm so groggy, as I approach the peephole. Its an elderly lady hollering for John to let her in.

I ease the door open with the chain still on. "There isn't anyone named John here Ma'am." I look around behind her, but there is no one around.

"Please John, let me in. I'm cold." She begs.

I lift the chain, and slowly step outside. "Ma'am let me help you to the office." I quickly look around wondering if I'm being setup for someone to murder me. I have a very active imagination, and I'm in a strange place.

I quickly get her to the lobby, as my mind races. I don't even get to ring the desk bell before a big older man comes out from behind the counter.

"Francine! I've been sick out of my mind hollering for you." He puts his arms around her, and soothes her with quiet words.

I don't want to interrupt, but I'm so tired. "Excuse me Sir, is she okay?" I ask quietly.

"Oh dear, yes thank you." He holds out his hand. "I'm John, and this is my wife Francine. She wonders off sometimes, and forgets where she's at. Thank you so much for bringing her back."

"I'm Carrie, and you're welcome, but I really need to get back to bed now."

"Please come by the diner down the way in the morning, and breakfast will be on the house."

"It may be lunchtime before I get up." I smile through my yawn at his kindness.

"That will be just fine. My grandson Chance runs the place. You just tell him John sent you."

I say goodnight, and head back to bed hoping for a peaceful sleep.

I wasn't far off on the lunchtime guess. I wake up around eleven thirty to Justine whistling in the shower.

"I need coffee." I mumble trying to get my eyes to adjust.

Justine comes out of the bathroom all cheery looking. "Good morning sunshine." She plops down on my bed.

"Coffee." I slip on my wrinkled clothes, put a hair tie on my wrist, and step out the door to head for the diner.

Justine rushes after me. "You're not going to shower first?" She is laughing at me because she knows I'm a bitch without my coffee.

"Coffee." I mumble as we enter the diner, and take a seat in a corner.

"What can I get for you ladies?" A cheery looking little blonde teenager asks.

"I'd like eggs, bacon, toast, and pancakes." Justine smiles.

"You Miss?"

"Coffee." I mumble.

"Don't worry, she knows more than one word sentences, but only after she has her coffee." Justine is laughing at me while I scowl back at her.

After the waitress fills my coffee for the third time I finally feel human enough for conversation. "You sleep like a log, don't you? Did you even hear anything last night?"

"Not a thing. I needed that sleep." Justine smiles at me.

"You didn't even know I was gone."

"What are you talking about?"

I explain the whole story about Francine, and why I'm so out of it this morning, or afternoon.

"No shit!"

"Excuse me hon." I wave the waitress over. "Can I order something to eat now?"

"Sure, but breakfast is over. Would you like some lunch?"

"A bacon cheeseburger, fries, and a sprite please."

"Sure thing." She practically skips away.

"Damn, she sure is cheerful." I laugh.

"So, this grandson of his, where is he?" Justine stands up, and tries to see behind the counter into the kitchen.

"Sit down, will you. I just want to eat something, then maybe shop around town for a little while. Do some exploring, or something."

"Drink! You owe me a drink, and I saw a bar across the street."

"Its early afternoon, are you crazy." I laugh.

"So, its five o'clock somewhere."

"Food, shower, shopping, then we will get our drink on." I shake my head as the girl puts my food down. "Thank you." I say to the waitress then dig in because I am starving.

"Hey!" I slap Justine's fingers when she steals a fry. "Mmmm, ah god, this cheeseburger is so good." I mumble with my mouth full.

"Well, well, well." Justine's eyes are looking behind me.

"Carrie?"

I almost choke on my cheeseburger from the voice. Deep and strong, sending shivers down my spine. I slowly swallow, and wipe my mouth before I turn in my seat.

My eyes go from his boots all the way up to his beard, but when I get to his eyes, I just stare. He is handsome in a rugged kind of way. He has a scar on the left side of his nose that looks like it has been broken before.

"Carrie?" He asks again, as if confused.

"Yes." I feel like I lost my voice. I feel flushed, and over heated all in a matter of seconds.

"Hi, I'm Chance. My Grandpa called, and told me what you did for my Nana. I wanted to thank you personally." He holds out his hand.

I grab his hand, and its rough with callouses. I feel tingles run up my arm, as my eyes are glued to his eyes.

"Please, sit down, and tell us about your Nana." Justine jesters for him to sit down beside me.

I scoot over automatically, but continue to hold his hand.

He sits beside me with his thigh touching mine, and slowly pulls his hand free of mine as he smiles. "Rough night?" He reaches up, and tweaks my hair.

I then remember my rats nest that I didn't comb. I grab the hair tie off my wrist and pull my hair into a sloppy ponytail, and let it hand down my back. "Shit." I laugh. "I had a long day at work, and then a long drive."

"She needed coffee before she could function." Justine interrupts.

"Where are you from?" His eyes are on me.

"Ohio. Now, please tell me about your Nana. She seemed scared last night, so I couldn't not help her." I change the subject because I don't want to talk about my lonely life back home.

"She has dementia. The last year has been rough, but my Grandpa takes care of her, and I take care of them. Some days are better than others. Last night was not one of those better ones. We have an alarm that goes off when she leaves the building, but the battery went dead, and I forgot to check it last night before I went home." He turns his eyes away for a second.

"Well, you're only human, and I'm sure they are grateful for you." I touch his hand not even realizing it until he looks down at my fingers. I snatch my hand back.

"Thank you, but I'm the one who is grateful." He stands up quickly. " Lunch is on me, and I hope you ladies enjoy your day."

My eyes follow him until he is out of sight.

"Wow." Justine murmurs.

I jerk my head around to her staring at me. "I need a shower." I hurry up and finish my food, and leave a nice tip on the table before I rush out of the diner.

"You should totally ride that ride." Justine blurts out as soon as the hotel door shuts behind her.

"What?" I gather up some clothes.

"Chance."

"Huh?" I turn toward the bathroom pretending ignorance.

"Stop acting dumb." She laughs, as I close the bathroom door in her face.

I strip, and get in the shower. As I'm washing I start remembering the way he looked. Tall, rough, a little soft in the belly, but still hot. Dark hair, beard, and a crooked smile.

I quickly finish before I start touching places that haven't been touched in years other than by my own hand.

I throw on my jeans, tee shirt, and flip flops and sit on the bed. "Will you braid my hair, its to hot to wear down."

"Sure, then we need to go shopping for some outfits for a night on the town. Oh yeah girl." She quickly finishes up before we head out.

There are a few clothing shops we try out, but decide to move on to another one. "Class and Sass."

"That sound interesting." We walk in and the lady goes straight to Justine.

"Hello, I'm Crystal. What can I help you find today?" A brick house stacked blonde holds out her hand.

"Well, we want to have a night out on the town. Something sexy, and fun." Justine follows her to a rack of dresses.

"This is cute, and short enough to be sexy." Justine holds it up to herself. "What do you think Carrie?"

"Its hot, but the blue one would go better with your skin tone."

"Yes!" She quickly grabs a blue one. "Do you have a dressing room?"

"Sure, this way." Crystal leads her to the back.

"Hi, Carrie right?" The young waitress comes up behind me.

"Yes, hello." I smile at her.

"I'm Emily, Chance's niece from the diner."

"Hi Emily, I love your boots." She is wearing pink cowgirl boots.

"Thanks, find anything yet?" She jesters around.

"Oh, I'm sorry dear, I don't think we have your size." Crystal says behind me.

I turn around and she is looking at me like I'm a cow. "Excuse me?" I'm thrown off by her rude, bitchy behavior.

"There's a plus size store for big women down the road."

"Wow." I start laughing in her face.

"Crystal, you're a bitch!" Emily says just as Justine comes out of the dressing room to show us the dress on her.

"Don't worry about it sweety, I've dealt with women like her for years."

"What the hell did I miss?" Justine walks up to us.

"You look beautiful, but I'm going to wait outside." I start to turn.

"Wait a damn minute. Now you know you need to tell me before I start kicking ass and ask again later." Justine looks over to Emily for answers.

"Crystal is a bitch, and she was rude to your friend." Emily crosses her arms over her chest.

"Is that so?" She quietly says as she walks up to Crystal.

"Not worth it. Lets go." I know my friend will kick her ass if I don't get us out of here.

"Fine, but I suggest you move out of my way before I flatten your ass." Justine grabs the dress and pulls it up over her head, and tosses it on the floor as she heads to the dressing room for her clothes.

I want to laugh at everyone's face when Justine lets it all hang out. I wink at Emily to let her know its all good.

When we get outside Emily laughs so hard she bends over at the knees. "Did you see her, that was badass girl!" She high fives Justine.

We shop a few more hours, and pick up some sexy dresses.

"Lets go to the hotel then we need to go get a drink." I smile just thinking about it.

"I'll meet you two there." Emily turns to leave.

"What? Wait, how old are you girl?" I don't want a teenager following us to a bar.

"I'm twenty two."

"No fucking way!" I laugh until she pulls out her drivers license, and sure enough she is twenty two.

"I thought you were a damn teenager." Justine blurts.

"Ask Uncle Chance, he'll tell you."

"Um, no... Lets just go to the bar," I stammer as my heart rate picks up.

"Okay, but I will meet you there. I have to change and stuff."

"Okay Em, see you soon." I holler as we head to the hotel.

"What the hell is wrong with you? Every time that mans name comes up you blush." She wiggles her eyebrows at me.

"I'm going to change." I grab my bag then rush into the bathroom before Justine can question me more.

I put on the teal colored dress that comes just above my knees. I love it except the front is a little too revealing on my boobs.

"Justine, can you help me with the front of this?" I open the door.

"Wow, hot momma. Its perfect, help with what?" She walks around me.

"My boobs are all in your face in this dress!" I laugh at her smiling.

"Duh! Men love boobs."

"Smart ass." I mutter.

Justine grabs the hair clip out of my hair, and it all falls down to my ass. "Hey, I can't dance with my hair down, It will be to hot." I protest, and try to grab it back.

"I'll braid it for you later."

"Fucking hell, just get dressed. I need a drink,"

When she disappears behind the bathroom door, I grab another hair clip, and put it back up.

She bitches all about it clear to the bar. She wiggles her little ass into a booth with her short white dress.

"Any shorter, and everyone would get a view." I laugh when she sticks her tongue out at me. "I'll be right back with some starter drinks."

I order four shots of whiskey, a vodka cranberry, and a pitcher of margaritas.When it all gets set on the table Justine's eyes jump to mine.

"You're going to clean up the puke if we drink all that." She grabs a shot.

"If I'm going to drink then I may as well go for it." I slam my first shot. "Fuck, that shit burns."

We manage all four shots, and I drink the vodka cranberry before we decide to hit the dance floor.

We dance, laugh, and goof off for three songs before I've had enough. "Okay, I'm done!" I feel a little tipsy.

"Not yet pretty lady, dance one song with me."

I turn to Chance, expecting him to be talking to Justine, but he is staring at me.

"Carrie, the man wants a dance." Justine pushes me into his arms, as she walks off the dance floor.

"Are you shy Darlin'?" He chuckles in my ear.

I feel goosebumps all the way down my body. "I just thought you were um, well, I thought you were asking Justine to dance." I shrug my shoulders, a little embarrassed.

"I don't flirt with married women." His warm breath slides across my ear.

"Oh, is that what your doing? Are you flirting with me Chance?" I giggle, feeling a little tipsy.

"Hell yes, a pretty lady and a dance floor that gets you in my arms. So far so good." He nips my ear with his teeth.

My head snaps back, and I see lust in his eyes. My body is on board because without even thinking my hips move forward. "Damn." I whisper as I stare into his eyes feeling my cheeks go hot.

"The song ended. Do you want to keep dancing or get a drink?" His hand squeezes my waist as I feel his hardness push against my stomach.

"Drink, I think I need a drink." I blurt out when he chuckles.

He leads me with his hand, just above my butt, back to my table where Justine is smiling ear to ear.

"Enjoy the dance?" She scoots over for me.

Chance slides in beside me until his thigh pushes against mine.

I feel heat run clear through my body. I grab my glass, and fill it to the rim with a margarita. I take a long drink before I take a deep breath.

"So, you ladies never did say where you were heading." He fiddles with my hair clip as I lean back against the booth.

"Just an adventure from our everyday lives. We had vacation time, and we needed a break from work." Justine refills her our glasses.

"What kind of work?"

"Well, we work in a warehouse. Boring shit to pay the bills. Carrie however, writes novels.”

I choke a little on my drink. “Justine, I thought we agreed to leave work at home.”

“I don’t consider that apart of you’re job because you love to write so......?” She leaves the sentence for me to finish.

“What do you write?”

“She writes smutty romance.”

“Justine! Damn, you’re just a big mouth tonight.” I laugh.

“Smutty huh? Now I have to read some. Do you have a pen name?”

“Just look up Carrie Newton.” I smile as I finish my margarita.

“Newton, like a fig newton with the fruity delicious center?” He quietly says as his lips graze my ear. “I could eat that all day.” I feel his fingers lightly run up my inner thigh. “I like your dress.” He says casually out loud as if I’m not squeezing his hand with my inner thigh muscles. I don’t know if I’m trying to hold his hand between my legs, or stop myself from cumming where I sit.

“Thank you.”I go to grab the pitcher, and realize its empty.

“I need to go check on my Nana, and Grandpa before they go to bed. Would you ladies like to come along for some more refreshments at my place? Its just down the road from the hotel.” He squeezes my thigh then brings his hand up to my neck.

“We would love to Chance, you lead the way.” Justine grabs my hand, and squeezes.

I wobble a little as I stand up, and I giggle because I’m feeling quite tipsy.

“Easy sweetheart. Wait here for just a few minutes.” Chance heads up to the bar, and returns a few moments later with a brown paper bag. “Come on, I got burgers.”

We step outside in the fresh cool air. I feel so good in this moment that I begin to twirl around slowly.

“Feeling good?” Chance smiles.

“I’m feeling playful.” I wink, and pinch his butt.

He grabs me up, and throws me over his shoulder laughing.

“Oh damn, my head is spinning. Put me down!” I yell out in a rush.

"Shit, I'm sorry Carrie." He puts me down.

I lean down, and take a few deep breaths before I start laughing.

"You okay?" Justine puts her arm around me.

"Yeah, I think it was a close call." I stand up and look at Chance.

"We're here, come on in, and lets get you a cold wash rag." He leads us into his small cottage looking house. "The bathroom is this way Carrie, come here. Justine, make yourself at home." He pulls me into a small, but adorable bathroom with light blue walls.

He lifts me up, and sits me on the sink. I watch his arm muscles flex, as he reaches up to the top of a cupboard to get a washrag. He puts it under the cold water, as I continue to stare at his hands. He slowly wipes my face and neck. I stare up at his eyes as he runs the rag across the top o f my breasts. I see desire, and lust as my chest begins to rise faster with every breath I take.

"I want to taste your lips." His breath is warm against my neck when I feel his lips kiss my pulse.

I hear a whimpering sound come out of my mouth right before his mouth descends onto mine.His lips are so soft, and he coaxes my mouth open wider, as his tongue slides inside. I feel my ass slide toward the edge of the sink in order to get closer to him.

"Damn." His mouth slides onto my neck and he bites my skin.

I gasp out loud as I feel my panties become wetter.

"I have to go check on my Nana. Go eat something, and keep Justine company." He steps back a little. "Fuck, you're beautiful."

"What? Oh, okay." I blush.

I look down to where his eyes travel. My legs are open to him where my dress rode up to my panties, and he has to see the evidence of my desire. I sit up and pull my legs together.

He pulls me off the counter, and hands me the washrag.

"Kiss me."

He kisses my forehead. "Babe, if I kiss you again now, I'm going to fuck you against the sink. I need to get some cold air before I check on my grandparents. I'll be back." He turns, and leaves.

I'm still standing there when Justine comes in.

"Wow." She turns me toward the mirror.

My face is flushed, my eyes are glossy, and my neck has a love bite on it. "Holy shit." I finish wiping my face off, and head to the living room.

"You want a drink?" Justine pulls a few beers out of Chance's refrigerator.

"Sure, but I think I'll eat a cheeseburger first." I need to sober up a little.

We sit down on the couch together, and I eat but she continues to drink. "For someone who doesn't drink, you sure are slamming them down." I giggle at her.

"They are going down smooth!" She leans toward me, and her laughter is contagious.

She drinks three more before Chance gets back, and she is drunk as hell.

"Ladies, did you miss me!" He flops down in his big recliner chair.

"Damn, you are hot!" Justine slurs, as she leans back onto the couch.

"Thanks." Chance winks at her in her drunken state.

"She doesn't get to relax very often." I smile at her.

"You're the best Carrie, love you." She mumbles as her head falls to the side.

I hurry up and grab her half empty beer before it falls out of her hand. She is out cold.

"Are you two close?" He smiles at her passed out form when I cover her up.

"Yes, she has been my best friend since the day she saved my life." I look up at him, and his eyebrow is raised in question. "Maybe I'll tell you about it someday." I shake my head not wanting those memories to surface.

"I hope so." He grabs my hand and pulls me toward his lap.

"I don't know how long we are going to be here, we may be gone tomorrow." I quietly say, as I stare into his eyes.

"I know, but I want you to remember me because I know damn well that I won't be forgetting you." His mouth urgently crushes mine.

I stiffen for a second before I become completely weightless in is arms. My body responds with a rush of tingles down to my core. His tongue thrusts inside when I gasp. His hands slide down to my ass, and he grips me hard against him. I cry out, and grind myself down onto his hardness.

"Carrie." His lips slide down onto my neck. "We need to slow down." He groans his hot breath against my skin causing goosebumps to cover my arms.

"Please." I beg as my skin feels like its on fire with need. I reach down, and unfasten his jeans to reach inside. I stroke him into my palm. "Please."

"Oh fuck, Carrie." He pushes up harder against my hand while I use my other hand to jerk his jeans down enough to release him completely.

"Wow, oh god. Yes, please. I need you so bad." I raise myself up over his cock, pull my underwear to the side, and slam myself down onto him. I'm dripping all over him. I cover his mouth, as we both cry out with pleasure.

"Fuck!" He moans, as he goes out of control. His hands squeezes my hips, as he pushes up into me over, and over.

I pull my mouth off of his, and bite his shoulder hard when my body pours my orgasm all over his cock. "Chance." I feel like I'm blacking out from the pleasure my body is receiving.

Its too much for him to handle as well because I feel his hotness pump up inside of me.

I bury my face into his neck as my emotions well up. I can't stop the tears from coming. I squeeze my eyes tight, as I hold onto him tightly.

"Carrie?" He whispers my name while rubbing his hand down my head and back in a comforting touch.

"Thank you." I slowly pull my face out of his neck, and kiss across his cheeks ti his mouth.

"Hey, are you okay baby?" His face shows concern when he wipes my tears off my face.

"Yes."

"Talk to me, please."

"I really like you Chance." I ease myself up, and hold out my hand. "Take me to your bed."

"Come on."

He takes me upstairs, and shuts us in his room. He strips us both naked without speaking, grabs my hand, and pulls me onto the bed.

I snuggle into his arms with my head on his shoulders.

"I like you here." I feel his lips on my head.

We lay quietly for awhile before I feel okay enough to speak. "Three years ago I was walking alone at night because I couldn't sleep. I had been divorced for a year, and I was trying to get my life together. I had my headphones on listening to an audio book when I was shoved to the ground from behind. He told me if I screamed that he would kill me. He shoved what I thought was a gun to the back of my head while he tried to jerk my pants down." I feel Chance's arms hold me tighter, but he doesn't speak. "The next thing I know the weight of his body is gone, and there is a woman standing over the man with a baseball bat and he is all bloody. She grabbed me up, we left, and have been best friends ever since."

"Justine."

"Yes."

"Why did you thank me?" He pulls my chin up to see into my eyes.

"Your the first man that I have felt any desire for, to let touch me, and want to touch me." I lay my head back down to nuzzle his chest. He smells so good. "I'm very attracted to you, not just your body, but the way you make me feel safe enough to let my guard down." I kiss his chest. " I thanked you for being you."

"Your welcome. I'm glad I'm not the only one who is feeling this connection between us. Get some sleep."

I must have dozed off sometime because sunlight is peeking through the window.

I stretch myself awake feeling like I slept like a baby. Reality kicks in when I feel the tenderness between my legs. I instantly stiffen.

"Please don't regret it."

I jerk my head around to Chance's soft voice, and sinfully sexy eyes. I sit up, and pull the sheet over my breasts, as I feel my cheeks heat up. "I could never regret you,

I just...   I've never done this before. Not sex, but this." I realize I'm babbling, I close my mouth, and bite my lip.

"Shhh, I know what you mean." He sits up, reaches over, and pulls me into his lap causing the sheet to fall away. "Give me this." He reaches down to line himself up with me. "Look at me." He watches my eyes when he slides himself into me slowly an inch at a time.

The feeling of him filling me is extraordinary. "Oh god." My eyes roll to the back of my head in pleasure.

"Look at me." His voice pulls my eyes right back to his face. He rolls us over, and continues to slide in and out of me painfully slow.

The care he is showing me is overwhelming. I've never felt such intensity before. He makes me truly believe he owns my body. He is consuming me with the desire in his eyes. I feel the pressure building inside of me.

"Come apart with me Carrie." He groans with the first hot sensation of his release.

His heat causes me to go over the edge and release my own build up. My orgasm explodes out of me from his tenderness, his voice, and the raw emotion on his face.

"Chance." I pull his full weight onto me with his release. I hold him tightly, not wanting to lose this connection.

When he finally eases off of me, he grabs my clutch purse off the floor. "Give me your phone."

I hand him my cellphone.

"This is my number." He clicks away then I hear his cellphone ring. "Now I have yours. Please don't disappear forever on me Carrie." He lays my phone down, and strokes my cheek with tenderness.

"I'm a grandmother!" I blurt out.

"So, are you worried that I'm too young for you?"

"Maybe." I mumble.

"I'm thirty four, single, no kids, and no secrets. I don't give a shit if your older than me. I know what I want." He cages me in.

"I can't have no more kids, I live alone, and I'm scared of the way you make me feel." I turn my head. "I fucking hate feeling vulnerable like this because I'm not a vulnerable woman any more, dammit! Why do I feel so damn emotional around you?"

I shove him up, and off of me. I need to get my shit under control because this is fucked up. I stand up frantically searching for my clothes.

"God dammit Carrie, do you think your the only one who is scared? I've never felt so out of control around anyone before." He pins me against the wall with his body caged all around me. "Just don't fucking walk out of my life as fast as you came into it. Please." His lips are touching my ear as he begs me to slow down.

My heart is racing, my lungs feel on fire from the loss of oxygen. "I need to slow down, this is too fast. I just met you, you have a life here, I have a life elsewhere. How does that work? I'm too... You're too.... Fuck, I don't know." I begin to panic.

"Carrie?" Justine is pounding on the bedroom door.

"Coming!" I ease my way out of his arms to get my dress off the floor. When I turn back around his eyes are begging me to stay. "I'll call you Chance. I just need some time. Please."

"Yeah, you do that." He sits down on the bed, and the last image I have, as I walk out, is him holding his head down in defeat.

Justine and I spend the rest of our two weeks traveling, getting drunk, and not discussing my stupid broken heart. I try not to remember his tenderness, crooked smile, or his ability to make me feel more than I have felt in years. Its crazy how the heart attaches itself while the mind can't comprehend something happening so fast.

Weeks after we've been back home I still feel like I'm in a daze. Living everyday driving myself insane over the emotions that well up in me over the stupidest shit. I grabbed a cheeseburger for lunch, and when I went to take a bite I got overwhelmed with a memory of seeing his face for the first time. I tried to have a beer after work, and the memory of his lips on a bottle flashed in my mind. The lonely nights are the worst. Remembering the feel of him inside of me can make me feel paralyzed at times.

I'm getting more depressed, as the days go by. I deleted the first few text from Chance. I told myself that he is too young for me, that it was just a fling ,and it wasn't as real as I thought it was.

I've reached a month of hating myself for hurting him. The last text was from a few days ago, and I can't get it out of my mind. Eight words, eight lousy words, and I feel myself crumbling. 'Please tell me it was real for you'

I'm up half the night crying myself to sleep missing him. Its fucking insane having these emotions.

I never even hear my alarm go off for work, or Justine beating down my door until she rips the covers off, and drenches me in cold water.

"What the hell!" I scream.

"I've been calling, worried sick. You need to get up, you look like hell!" She grabs my face.

"I'm up. I was up really late. Oh god, my head hurts." I begin to strip as I enter the shower.

Ten minutes later I'm sitting on my bed in my bathrobe. I don't know what to say to Justine.

"Why!" Justine is so pissed her foot is tapping the floor. "You are so different, ever since our trip. Since Chance." She sits down beside me. "Just fucking talk to me Carrie, please. You're my best friend, and I'm worried about you." She grabs my hand.

"I told him about that night." I whisper, as a tear rolls down my cheek.

"You refuse to talk to anyone about that night, even me."

"I miss him so bad Justine. How can that be?" I'm so confused.

"Are you afraid he doesn't feel the same?"

"He sent me at least twenty texts. At first I refused to believe how I was feeling, then when the feelings wouldn't go away I was afraid it was too late, maybe he hates me by now. I don't know, this is so fucked up. I can't sleep, ever since that night he held me, I haven't slept worth a shit by myself." I lean my head on her shoulder. "Do you think he hates me by now? I feel like such a fucking coward."

"Can I see your phone?" She reads through all the texts that I didn't delete. "Was it real for you Carrie?" She quietly asks.

"Yes." I lean my head down, running my fingers into my hair.

"Call him."

"I can't dammit!" I stand with my back to her. "What if he has someone else by now?" I whisper in fear walking to the window. "Fuck!" I scream out, hating myself for sounding so weak.

"This isn't you Carrie. Where is the woman who became strong after her divorce. The one who doesn't take shit from anyone anymore." She is in my face now, and pissed.

"What?"

"Fucking woman up damn you!" She grabs my hand, and smacks my phone into it.

I stare at his number for a few moments trying to get my courage up. I growl in frustration at myself and hit dial while I hold my breath.

"Hello?"

My heart nearly hits the floor at the sound of his voice, and I make a whimpering sound.

"Carrie? Please, just talk to me."

I swallow past the lump in my throat to say the only words that matter in this moment. "It was real."

"Thank god."

The relief I hear in his voice causes me to lose my shit and choke back a sob when my ass hits the mattress.

Chance

Thirty four days of pure hell waiting. I thought I was a damn fool in falling for a woman who tossed me aside. The overwhelming relief of hearing her say it was real causes me to sit my ass down hard, as my legs give out.

"Give me your address Carrie." I can't chance not finding her, or losing her again now that I know she wants me.

"I just sent it to you."

"I'm coming for you, pack your bags, quit your job, I don't fucking care if I sound insane. You're mine, and no one is keeping me from you, not even you yourself."

"Chance?" She sounds scared.

"Do you want me?"

"Yes." I barely hear her whisper.

"Do you regret me?" I hold my breath.

"Never."

"I'm coming, by late tonight you will be in my arms. Life is too short to not take it with both hands."

"I'll be waiting." She says softly.

I need to finish up in the restaurant, talk to my Grandpa and Nana, then go get my woman. My heart is beating out of my chest, as I feel a big smile on my face. This is crazy, fucking crazy good.

"Wow, look at that."

I turn to Emily looking at me. I shove my cell back into my pocket. "What?" I shrug.

"That was Carrie wasn't it?" She hugs me. "Now maybe you will be easier to be around."

"I need to finish my shift, pack a bag, shit I need to talk to Sonny about taking over my shifts for a few days." I start toward the kitchen.

"Slow down Uncle Chance!" Emily grabs my arm. "Go pack a bag, and then go talk to Grandpa. I will talk to Sonny. I'm happy for you, I really liked Carrie."

"Am I crazy, I mean this is a once in a lifetime feeling for me. I can't be without her any longer." I begin to pace.

"Go, bring her back, and be happy. You are the sweetest man I know, and you deserve it." Emily hugs me tight.

"Thank you sweetheart."

My Grandpa just smiles at me when I explain it all to him. I know he understands the feeling by the way he looks at my Nana. They wish me well, and a safe return.

I finished my shift at the restaurant, and I've been on the road for about four hours.

I need to stop for a restroom break and some food. I pull into a gas station that has a Subway in it. I find a little table to eat at. Its been to long since I've heard her voice, so I decide to call her. Her phone goes to voice mail.

"Hey babe,its Chance. I just wanted to hear your voice, and to let you know that I'm halfway to you. I can't wait to have you in my arms." I'm a little disappointed that I didn't get to speak to her, but I know its only a matter of a few hours.

The drive seems to go on forever before I finally pull up in front of her apartment building. Its pitch black outside.

I send her a text to let her know I'm outside. I stand in front of her door with a bag in my hand. I've never been so nervous in all my life. I wait a few moments then knock. I wait, but still no answer. My heart begins to beat faster. What if she changed her mind? What if she doesn't want me here? My mind is going a mile a minute.

I pull up her number and call her.

"Hello." She sounds out of breath.

"Jesus, Carrie." I pull air into my lungs, and slowly release it. "I..."

"Are you here? Where are you?" She sounds a little frantic.

"I'm at your door." The sentence is barely out of my mouth when the door is pulled open revealing a dripping wet gorgeous woman in a bath towel that is barely covering her.

My eyes travel from her feet up to her thighs where a drop of water is slowly rolling down her leg. My eyes continue up until they rest on her cleavage, that is trying to bust free. I feel myself harden behind my zipper.

"Chance." Her beautiful mouth whispers my name as my eyes connect with hers. Her tongue peeks out, and she licks her lips.

I hear myself moan as I lose control. I have her against my body devouring her mouth, as my hand squeezes her ass to pull her tight against my aching cock. Its been forever since I've been inside of her.

I use my foot and kick the door shut behind us. I have her against the door with her legs around me in seconds. I stretch my palm wide under her towel on her ass, and use my fingers to touch lower.

"Please." She begs.

I lower her legs down to the floor. I pull her towel off, as I kneel in front of her. I put her leg over my shoulder, diving into her sweet pussy with my hungry mouth. I need her taste in my mouth as much as I need my next breath.

I can't comprehend what she is saying when she pulls my hair to keep me tight against her. I don't stop. I lick, I bite, and I suck her juices out of her. My chin is soaked as she screams through her orgasm. I can't stop. "More." I demand, as she slides down the door to the floor.

"I can't, oh god! Please."

I don't let up, I push her legs wider with my shoulders. My arm is across her hips, as my fingers spread her pussy open wider for my pleasure. I push two fingers up inside of her, and curl them to reach her pleasure spot. I bite down on her clit, and her pussy contracts then she gushes onto my chin. I bury my mouth in her opening to suck all of her down my throat.

Her mouth is open, but nothing is coming out but silent sobs. Her tears are real. "Chance." Her arm goes across her eyes.

I pull myself up her body, and flip us so she is sprawled across my chest with her face in my neck. I wipe my mouth then try to soothe her with kisses to her head.

"Please look at me." I need to see her eyes.

She leans up to look at me. "I missed you." She kisses me.

I just lay still, holding her, and soothing her by running my hands down her hair, and back while she kisses me.

She lays her head back down onto my chest still breathing hard. "This is crazy." I can feel her heartbeat through my shirt.

"Crazy good." I moan as I push my still hard body up.

"I want to taste you." She leans up into a sitting position across my hips. "Take your shirt off." She pulls the hem of my shirt out of my pants and I pull it over my head.

Her eyes are glued to my chest as she slowly leans down, and runs her tongue across my nipples, back and forth till she bites down on one.

"Fuck!" I moan at the amazing sensation that I've never experienced before.

"You like?" Her smile tells me that she likes my reaction.

I've fantasized about it, but never asked for it. "Bite me again." I let her see my desire for her to control my body, just this once.

"I want you to get up, strip down, then spread yourself out naked for me." She stands up above me with her juices still running down her thighs.

"I'll try my best, but baby you've got to know I will take over." I lean up, and bite her right on her plump pussy lips then lick her slit to soothe the ache.

"Oh god, just this once please." She tries to grab my hair to keep me at her pussy.

I quickly scoot back, and stand up out of her reach before I lose control, and take over completely. Before she gets her chance to do what she wants with my body. I'm on the edge of my control. I want to turn her over and fuck her senseless.

I strip my jeans, and boxers off in one motion. "Where?" I follow her finger to where her room is.

I climb on the bed, and spread myself out for her. I'm on my back with my legs up, and my feet flat on the bed.

She looks at me then opens her closet. My eyes follow her hands when she pulls out several scarves.

"Carrie." I growl because I know she wants to tie me up.

"Please." She leans over my face.

"Fuck! I'll try." I grit out as I lean up, and capture her nipple into my mouth sucking hard. My fist are clenched tight into the sheets to stop myself from grabbing her.

She is whimpering when she pulls back and squeezes her thighs together.

"Do I make you wet Carrie?" I follow her eyes as she ties my wrist to the headboard.

Her chest is rising faster as she looks down at my erection.

"Do you want to suck my cock?" I push my hips up in invitation even as she ties my ankles to the bed. I'm so fucking hard, and leaking cum out of my cock.

She slowly crawls between my legs and leans over my chest.

"Suck me." I bite out like an animal in heat.

She just smiles at me when she leans down for a kiss. She slowly licks my bottom lip, and pulls back when I try to take over the kiss.

I have to physically stop myself from pulling at the scarves on my wrist. I could break this fucking headboard, and just take over, but I know she wants to try this.

"Touch me dammit!" I'm begging just as much as I'm demanding.

She just keeps smiling at me with her eyes, as she continues to lick down my throat, and onto my chest. This slowness is agonizing, but the buildup is incredible. My hips rise up and nudge her ass. I can feel my cock push against her ass, but she leans out of my reach. I can feel her nipples rub onto my stomach when she begins licking my chest.

"Suck me Carrie, please put your mouth on me baby. I need you so bad." I dripping so much pre cum.

"Ahhh!" I throw my head back in ecstasy when her hot mouth engulfs my cock all the way to the back of her throat. "Fucking beautiful." I moan feeling like I've finally found heaven. She doesn't slow down. I feel myself loosing control from the sudden change of slowness to fast hard core sucking. I frantically raise my hips, fucking her mouth. "I can't last like this, you have to slow down baby or I will cum in your mouth."

She sticks a finger in her mouth as she sucks me. Her saliva runs out of her mouth down onto my balls.

"Carrie, oh god." My balls are tightening up when I feel her wet finger slide down to my ass. "No dammit!" I try to squeeze my ass cheeks together as I pull on my wrists. I'm so far gone that the pleasure/pain of her finger pushing into my ass causes me to holler out loudly when my cum shoots to the back of her throat.

"Mmmm hmm." She moans as she swallows me down. She licks every drop, as I pulse over and over into her mouth.

I feel her finger slowly pull free of my ass when I collapse back onto the bed.

When she leans forward to kiss me, I pull on the scarves. "Untie me, or I will break your fucking bed." My voice is so strained and low that she stares at me while untying my wrists.

She only gets one undone before I take over and rip the other three off. She is sitting back quietly, looking a little nervous.

I feel like a lion in a cage who has just been set loose. No one has ever touched my ass before. I'm so pissed, but so turned on from the pleasure she gave me.

"Did you enjoy yourself Carrie?" I growl grabbing her waist, and flip her onto her stomach. I crawl up onto her, pinning her down.

"Yes." She says softly.

"My turn." The raw need in my voice is unmistakable.

"Chance, I....."

"Shhh." I pull her hips up off the bed, and spread her legs apart.

She is in front of me with her face down on the sheets and her ass in the ass for my viewing. I slowly begin to rub my fingers across her slit through her juices. She is soaking wet.

Everything she did to me turned me on. I need sometime to get hard again, so I plan on slowly torturing her till she begs me for it.

"Did you enjoy yourself?" I slowly gather her juices and rub them over her ass. I feel her stiffen as I continues to slaver her wetness onto her ass.

"Chance?" She sounds nervous, but turned on.

"Did you Carrie?" I chuckle a little at her nervous voice while she pushes her ass back against my fingers.

"Yes!" She moans as I push just the tip inside of her.

"Have you ever been taken here before?" She is so fucking tight.

"Not really, oh god, no I haven't."

I feel myself hardening at her words. "Someday soon, but not right now. I need to feel your sweet pussy gripping my cock tight." I pump myself a few times before I slam inside of her heat.

"Jesus fucking god, oh fuck!" She cries out. "Its been so long."

I can't slow down, I can't think about anything, but the tightness, the softness, and the pure pleasure of her sweet pussy's death grip on my cock. I slam into her over, and over.

"I need you to touch yourself Carrie, I'm so close."

"Chance!" Her orgasm soaks me, and I'm so far gone I didn't even notice she was already working herself.

I gather her juices, and push my finger partially inside of her ass causing another orgasm, as I fill her with my cum. Her pussy is contracting and squeezing me so tight.

I lean my head down on her back to catch my breath. I'm still holding her up by the waist so she don't collapse. My finger is still partially in her ass. I stare at it and slowly pull it free, fascinated by the muscles squeezing ,as if to keep me inside.

I lay onto my back, pulling her with me. She is in a daze. I pull in big gulping breaths to slow my heart down.

"I want to experience that with you someday." She squeezes me tightly.

"I want that too. I want everything with you."

We lay quietly for awhile then I hear her lightly snoring. This intense pull to be with her, the over whelming need to not give her up, and the fast beat of my heart every time she enters my mind, is why I'm here.

I've never experienced this before. I've dated, cared, and even tried to be in a relationship before, but this is not something I can give up. Its always been casual until now. Now its an intense feeling to make her happy above anything else.

Sometime later I wake up, and notice my arm is stiff. Its Carrie's head on my arm. My fingers are tingling as I move them. I ease my arm out, and go in search of the bathroom. This is a cute little apartment that I didn't notice when I got here.

I notice the clock in the bedroom when I return to her sleeping peacefully. Its already one in the afternoon. I grab some clothes out of my bag by the door, and head for the shower.

I decide to make her some afternoon breakfast when I enter the kitchen. The rolls are coming out of the oven when I feel arms slide around me.

"Careful, the pans hot." I turn around after moving away from the hot oven.

"Wow, you cooked and I smell coffee." She leans up to kiss me.

"I'm honored that I got a kiss before you reached for the coffee." I smile as she pours herself a cup.

"I usually don't even speak before I have coffee." She takes a sip, and the expression on her face is content.

"Damn, I must be special." I pull her out a chair. "Eat up."

"You are." She holds my stare before she sits down.

"Don't look at me like that, or you will be my breakfast." I let her see my desire.

She turns back to the table. "Wow you made eggs, bacon, and cinnamon rolls." She fills her plate.

"I figured you would be hungry when you got up since you had a hell of a work out last night." I see her swallow, as a blush runs up her neck.

We eat in silence for awhile before I broach the subject of returning to my home. My grandparents need me, and I can't be gone too long.

"Carrie, I need you to know that I would love to have the time to take this slow, but I don't have that luxury. I'm needed back home, so I need to know if you still want to go with me." I grab her hands, and kiss them.

She stands up and straddles my lap in just my t shirt, and nothing else. "I'm scared that this is all a dream. I'm scared that these emotions I feel for you are going to get me hurt, that someday you'll change your mind, that I'm not enough. Most of all I'm scared of losing you if I don't take this chance." She lays her head on my shoulder.

"I want you to be sure. You don't have to do this now if you're not ready. We'll make this work baby." I rub her back for comfort.

"I packed my bags already. I'm scared, but I'm doing this with you."

"What all do you need to do before we can leave?" I smile so big that my cheeks feel like they are going to split.

"I need to see Justine, stop at the bank, and call my boss. I'll deal with the rest later. On our way back to Mississippi I need to stop in Tennessee to speak to my daughter."

"Your daughter lives in Tennessee?"

"Yes, with her husband, daughter, and lots of animals. She's a vet, and they run a clinic."

"Nice, will I get to meet her?"

"Of course, and I haven't seen her in a few months."

"Does she know anything about me?" I hold my breath hoping she has mentioned me to her family.

"I told her that I met someone special while on vacation, but I didn't know where it was going. She calls me a couple of times a week, and she heard the sadness in my voice."

"Babe." I touch her cheek to get her eyes to meet mine.

"I wish I would have answered you sooner. I was so confused, and worried that I was just a fling. I'm still worried a little, I guess."

"We need time to get to know each other better. We will be living at my little cottage house for awhile. I need to be close to my grandparents."

"I love your house, well what I saw of it." Carrie laughs, and blushes at the same time.

"I told my Grandpa what I was doing. Do you know what he said to me?"

"What?" She kisses my lips.

"The heart doesn't lie son. He was staring at my Nana like she was everything.

I've always wanted to know the feeling, and now I'm getting the chance." I kiss her softly.

"You're hard." She moans, as she moves around on my lap. "You're mine Chance." She reaches down into my sweats, and pulls my cock out far enough to line herself up, and slide down onto me.

I raise my hips, and slide my sweats down a little farther, ensuring nothing gets in the way of feeling her. "Ride me." I can't stop myself from pushing hard up inside of her.

Its fast, and out of control. I feel my balls tighten up. My orgasm can't be stopped. I push her shirt up, and suck her nipple into my mouth, as I flick her clit. She explodes around me, as I spill inside of her.

"Fuck yes!"

"Carrie!"

We hold each other for awhile before Carrie decides she wants a shower.

"Want me to join you?" I nip her shoulder.

"Are you trying to kill me?" She laughs

"We'll never get on the road if I join you. Are you sore?"

When she stands up I see her flinch. "A little, but its the best kind of sore." She leans down, and kisses me, taking my breath.

"Go shower." I smack her ass when she walks away.

I get cleaned up, and start washing up the dishes when the doorbell rings. I open the door to Justine, and an older gentleman.

"Hey Justine, come on in. Carrie is in the shower, but she'll be out soon." I smile as I step back ,and let them in.

"So, its true then." The older gentleman is pointing at Carrie's suitcases by the couch.

"Alex, I told you not to come here. Chance, this is Alex."

"Carrie's husband." The guy says holding out his hand.

"Ex husband, for years now. Alex, what are you doing here?" Carrie walks up beside me looking pissed.

"Are you really moving away?" Alex totally ignores me while stepping up into Carrie's personal space sounding sad.

"Yes, I'm moving to Mississippi with Chance. I'll even be closer to Alexa now. Why are you here?" She steps closer to me.

"I overheard Justine talking about it with her husband at the grocery store."

"Eavesdropping more like it." Justine mutters aloud.

"Can we talk in private for a moment? Please, Carrie?"

I feel my muscles stiffen. I don't like this guy. He is acting all caring , and I don't buy it. Every step he gets closer to Carrie she steps back.

"I'm with Chance, and Justine is my best friend, so anything you have to say, you can say right here." Carrie edges closer to me.

I put my arm around her, pulling her into my side.

Alex instantly goes from calm, and sincere to tight lipped, and pissed. "You're young boy toy will grow tired of you soon enough. You never could keep a man happy." Alex growls at Carrie then turns, and slams the door behind him.

"Good riddance." Justine says to the door. " Are you okay Carrie?"

"Yeah, I just don't get it. Why now? I haven't spoken to him in years. He tried calling for awhile then quit when I wouldn't answer. Why the hell is he doing this now?"

"You have a man now honey. He never cared before because you've been single this whole time." Justine shrugs her shoulders.

"Was he always abusive to you?" I ask her, and she stiffens in my arms.

"I'm going to help myself to some breakfast. Talk to him Carrie." Justine squeezes her shoulder on her way to the kitchen.

"Come here." I pull her to the couch.

We sit quietly for a few moments. I just wait her out.

"At first it was small things, like telling me my ass was too big for certain clothes. It was always in private, then as time went by he slowly got worse. After Alexa was born I never lost all the weight I gained, so he would go out and leave me at home all the time." She snuggles closer to me with her head leaning on my chest. "The first time in public was when we got invited to a co workers barbecue. I finally talked him into going. I hadn't been out anywhere as a woman instead of a mom in a long time, so I got all dressed up. I felt so good about myself for the first time in a long time." She sets up to the edge of her couch and rubs her hands down her face, and takes a deep breath.

I squeeze her hand for support. I want her to be able to confide anything in me. To trust me enough to be vulnerable.

"I had a few drinks with the other women, and we were all standing around laughing. One of the women suggested that we join in on all the dancing. So as a group we all started dancing. We were having so much fun, and it felt so good. My drink was empty, so I went over to the coolers to get another one. When I turned around Alex was standing behind me looking pissed off. He asked me if I was ready to go home, and I said no. I asked him to please come dance with me first." She lowers her head into her hands.

I rub her back to let her know I'm here with her. I can see her struggling with her emotions.

"He grabbed my arm so tight." She is physically rubbing her arm with the memory. "He said why the hell would he want to dance with someone who already showed her fat ass,and tits to everyone else. He said my dress made me look like a whore who wanted to be fucked. That's when I noticed everything was quiet. The music had stopped and everyone was staring." I can see her discreetly wiping her eyes.

"No one did anything, and I felt so alone. Everyone just went back to what they were doing. I never felt the same after that. I still stayed married to that asshole for ten more years. My daughter was grown, and married by the time I got the will power to leave him. After I met Justine that night she helped me believe in myself. Its been four years since my divorce was final, but seeing him again with that anger in his voice brought back some horrific memories."

"Come here baby." I pull her back against me into my arms. "For his sake he best just stay away, or the next time I see him I'm going to smash his face in." The fucking anger I feel for what he put this wonderful woman through is enough to make me explode. I'm trying to stay calm for her. I'm glad I didn't know all this before that fucker shower up.

"My hero." She smiles a sad smile.

"Damn right baby. No one will ever treat you like that again. I mean it Carrie."

"Thank you."

"I'm not just a cook." I want her to know the real me.

"What all are you Chance, besides mine?" She snuggles into my chest.

"I'm a well trained Marine. I didn't sign back up because my family needs me. My grandparents lost their daughter, and the only son they ever had was a real piece of shit who left me with them to raise. I owe them everything, so I help with them, and I helped with Emily. I'm a protector Carrie, its what I was born to be. Those I care about will always have me until my last breath, and that includes you." I lean down and softly kiss her lips.

"What did you do in the Marines?" She slides her lips down my jaw, and I can feel her breath on my skin.

"I specialized in explosives, and hand to hand combat. It was some of the best times, and the worst times of my life. It helped make me the man I am today. The Marines, and my grandparents." I grab her hand, and lay it on my heart.

"I'm grateful for you, and for all of them. Thank you for your service honey."

As a veteran, being thanked for my service is not needed, but it is appreciated. I do it because its who I am.

Her mouth reaches up and captures mine in a hot searing kiss. I lean up over her to deepen the kiss.

"Amen sister!" Justine comes in, and plops down beside Carrie causing me to pull back. "I'm going to miss you everyday."

The women grab a hold of each other.

"Phone calls." Carrie mumbles into Justine's shoulder.

"Letters." Justine says at the same time.

"Vacations."

"Videos."

The ladies are crying, and making plans already to see each other.

"Don't worry about the apartment because I have a replacement for you." Justine wipes the tears off Carrie's cheeks.

"Already? Really?"

"Yep, I'm pushing the two oldest out of the nest."

"I bet Greg is loving that, he'll be able to chase you around the house more now."

"The man is already insatiable, he's going to kill me now."

"What a way to go!" I wiggle my eyes at Carrie.

"Its true Chance, my husband is always trying to get in my pants." Justine laughs.

"He sounds like a man I could get along with well. You two will have to come visit us as much as possible."

"I have two more weeks vacation next month. You keep us a room available, and we'll be there. Now, I really have to go before I cry again. I love you Carrie, be happy."

"I love you too." They hug really tight one more time.

"Drive safe." Justine pulls me into a hug. "Take good care of my girl Chance, or even the Marines won't be able to save you." She turns and walks out the door with tears in her eyes.

"She means that doesn't she?" I pull Carrie against my chest.

"Yes. She was a sniper in the special forces for the Army years back. The woman is a deadly weapon herself."

"I'm surprised your ex is still alive." I say in amazement.

"Me too." Her laugh is beautiful.

I settled everything with my bank, my job, and my landlord before we hit the road in our separate vehicles so I have my own transportation when we arrive.

I listen to soothing love songs all the way to Tennessee to see my daughter. It helps me remember why I'm taking this leap of faith with Chance.

I pull over to a small diner on the highway about twenty miles from my daughters house. I need to use the bathroom, and get my nerves under control so I can decide what I'm going to say to Alexa.

She knows about Chance, but she doesn't know I'm moving to be with him. I know she will understand but I'm still nervous.

We meet behind my truck, and his arms come around me. "Are you okay?" His smile helps calm me. I breath him in.

"Yes, just need the bathroom, and something to drink."

"I'll order for us, you go on to the bathroom." He kisses me. "Breathe baby."

I watch him go to the counter while I head to the ladies room. I take care of my bladder then as I am washing my hands my phone begins to vibrate.

"Shit." I decline the incoming call from Alex. I still don't understand why after all these years he would give a shit now. It pisses me off that he is even trying. If it wasn't for the fact that we have a child together I'd delete his ass from my contacts. I take a deep breath, and head out.

When I sit down at the table across from Chance I feel my phone begin vibrating again. I choose to ignore it.

"Whats wrong?" He grabs my hand. "You look like you just ate a sour candy."

"Normally, I'd say nothing because its just not worth my breath, but I don't want any secrets between us. Alex called me while I was in the bathroom."

The smile fades from his face. "What the hell does he want now?" He rubs his hand down his face.

"I don't know, I didn't answer." I smile at his little show of jealousy. "I have no desire to talk to him anyway. I haven't for years." I flip my palm over, and lace our fingers together. "I need one hundred percent honesty Chance. I won't tolerate anything less. I know its going to take time for us to learn everything about each other, so please feel free to tell me anything important now before we get to my daughters because she will drill you."

"You can ask me anything, and I will never lie to you. As for my past, its a little complicated when it comes to my parents, but everything else is pretty straight forward."

"Someday when your ready to tell me about your parents, I'll be all ears. For now I'll settle on hearing about any ex girlfriends in the town I'm moving to with you." I smirk when he has a blush run up his neck.

"I'm no monk that's for sure, but I never really did relationships. I told every woman I've ever been with that it was just straight up sex. I'm always honest about it. I tried dating a few times but it was just casual. My grandpa told me that when I met the right one that I would know, and that I would move heaven and earth to keep her." His eyes are warm and full of passion. "You're it for me." He turns my palm over and kisses it.

"Have you been with anyone since me?" I feel the moisture behind my eyes when I choke the question out. I have to know that I'm not in this alone.

"I can't even think of another woman, let alone touch one since you took my breath. When I saw you sitting in my diner, your hair a mess, no makeup, looking grouchy as hell, I knew then I'd never be the same. Then when you gave yourself to me , let your sweet pussy grip my cock, I knew I'd never let another woman touch me." I feel his tongue on my palm.

"Fuck that's hot." The waitress sits our drinks, and burgers down.

My face goes instantly red. Holy shit, I didn't even see her approach. She fans her face with her paper pad.

Chance just chuckles, but doesn't let me pull my hand free. "Thank you." He says for us both.

"Anytime sugar, and damn girl, you better hang onto this one." She winks, and walks away.

"Eat up." Chance bites into his burger, and moans. "Damn, this is delicious."

I'm still staring at his mouth feeling very overheated.

"Babe, that look right there will get you fucked hard." He reaches down, and adjust himself.

"What?" I hurry up and bite into my burger, moaning at the taste. "You're right this is delicious." I feel my panties dampen at his intense stare.

"You're so fucking beautiful." He says quietly.

I stare at him with my mouth full of burger wondering how I got so lucky to find him.

"Eat up." He continues to polish off his plate.

Twenty minutes later we're back on the road to Alexa's. The scenery is beautiful, and the miles pass by easily.

We pull down a long lane with a big sign that reads 'DESTINY'S ANIMAL KINGDOM VETERNARIAN SERVICES and SHELTERS'

I've barely gotten out of my truck when Alexa comes running out of the house. "Mom!" She throws her arms around me.

"My baby." I feel her against me. Its been a few months since I've seen her. The tears can not be stopped. I hold her till she pulls back to look at Chance.

"You must be Chance." My girl doesn't do handshakes, she pulls him into a big hug. He dwarfs her easily, my daughter is only five five. "Damn your tall compared to me, just like Nick. That's my husband, but he took Destiny down to the barn to help with the animals. You can meet them in a bit." She grabs Chance by the arm. "Mom, go see your granddaughter. I'll keep Chance company." She smiles at me sweetly.

"Alexa, don't start....."

"Go on honey, you know you want to see Destiny. We'll be fine." Chance kisses me, and winks.

"You we're warned." I laugh as I walk away.

I hurry toward the barn, smiling as I see Nick holding Destiny's foot to mount a horse. She heads on out into the field while her daddy stares after her.

"She sure has grown." I smile at his expression when he hears me.

"Carrie!" He hugs me tight. "How are you? Destiny is going to be so happy to see you."

"Let her ride for a bit so I can watch. She sure is amazing for a seven year old." The pride I feel inside makes my eyes water.

"Are you okay?" Nick pulls me under his shoulder for comfort.

"I miss this, seeing her more. Once every couple of months isn't enough." My heart aches for family.

"You know we have an extra room anytime you're ready. We'd love to have you here Carrie."

"I do need to talk to you two after I see my granddaughter. Thank you Nick, you're a great son in law." I pat his chest.

"You gave me the greatest gift of my life when you agreed to let me marry your daughter. I'd do anything for you."

"You already have, here she comes." I run out of the barn as Destiny slides out of the saddle. Nick takes the horse when I gather up my girl into my arms.

"Mamaw!"

"You looked great out there sweetheart, I missed you so much."

"Guess what?" She squeals. "I'm going to ride in the junior horse riding competition next month."

"Wow!"

She continues to talk excitedly, and fast about how she has to train to be ready.

I'm smiling so big when Chance walks in with Alexa.

"Who are you?" Destiny turns, and walks right up to Chance with her hands on her hips. "I like your beard."

"I'm Chance, and you definitely have to be Destiny." He holds out his hand.

"How do you know my name?" Her little hand is covered completely with his when they shake.

"Well, your Mamaw said you were beautiful, just like your mommy. You look just like her so I'm pretty sure I got it right." His smile is so genuinely sweet, and melts my heart.

"My mommy's beautiful because she looks just like my Mamaw." Her little hand rubs his beard.

"Yes, your Mamaw is very beautiful." His eyes find mine, and I think I see love reflected in them, but I turn just a little to stop myself from reading too much into it for now.

"I've got coffee on, and a cake cooling down if anyone is interested," Alexa invites us all back up to the house.

I watch Nick run with Destiny on his back giggling while Alexa tries to keep up. I feel Chance grab my hand, but the ache that hitches my heart pulls my eyes to him.

He is smiling, and laughing as if he has no care in the world. I can't help but wonder if I'm cheating him out of fatherhood. What if he regrets it later on, or resents me for it. He is only thirty four, and I might not be enough.

"You're killing me with those sad eyes baby." Chance stops, and pulls me into his arms. "What's going on in that pretty head of yours sweetheart?" His voice is filled with worry.

"I just...." I fist my hands into his shirt.

"One hundred percent honesty remember." He puts his forehead to mine to see into my eyes.

"I can't give you that." I turn to where Nick is with Destiny. "I don't want you to regret it later."

"Carrie, I know..."

"Shhh, please just don't." I kiss him to silence him.

I know he was going to say he was sure, but I need him to really be sure that I'm enough before he tells me he loves me. I see it in his eyes already, but I'm scared as hell to trust in that feeling just yet. I know my heart is full of love for him, but is that enough for me to believe it? I just don't know.

"Come on lets go get coffee, and cake." I pull my eyes away feeling like a coward.

We sit for a few hours discussing my plans to move in with Chance before we get ready to hit the road.

"Do you really have to go already mom? Its been so long." Alexa hugs me tight to her.

"I know baby, but now I'm only four hours away instead of eight. How about we start taking turns back in forth. You all come see us in two weeks then we will come to see Destiny in every competition we can get to. I love you so much baby girl." I can feel her tears on my shirt.

"Drive safe, and I love you too mom. I'm coming next weekend just because I need to know your good."

"Okay."

I bend down, and hug my granddaughter to me. I notice Alexa hugging Chance, and his facial expression shows that she is saying something in his ear.

"I love you Mamaw."

"You make my heart beat." I've been saying those words to her sense the day she was born, and I held her in my arms.

"Come on Chance, help me check the oil, and fluids in Carrie's truck so these ladies can talk." Nick takes Chance outside.

"Mom, I'm happy for you, and Chance seems like a really nice guy."

"But?"

"I'm always here if you need me, and a room is always open to you. That's all I'm saying."

"Thank you." I hug her tight to me one more time.

"Love is an emotional roller coaster."

"Alexa....I...."

"You wouldn't have brought him here otherwise. Hide it if you must, but you can't hide it from me."

"I'm scared. What if he doesn't feel as strongly, what if he changes his mind about kids, I can't give him that. My age compared to...." I feel tears.

"Breathe mom, don't let your fear get the best of you. One day at a time is all you can do. Trust him, and tell him how you feel. Get to know him even more before you freak out. I'm here day or night if you need me."

"I know your right, I just..."

"You are an amazing person."

"You are the amazing one baby girl. Thank you for easing my nerves."

Alexa grabs my hand and lays it on her stomach with tears in her eyes.

"Alexa?" I raise my eyes to hers.

"Shhh, just between us for a little while."

"Walk me out." I squeeze her hands in mine feeling so happy.

The hood of my truck is closed by Nick. "All good under the hood Carrie." Nick pulls me into his arms. "Drive safe, and call us when you arrive."

"Best son in law ever." I kiss his cheek, and hug him back. "Take care of my babies."

"Always."

Nick steps back to his little family, as I get into my truck.

Chance leans in my window, as I'm buckling up. "Drive safe baby, we're going home." He pulls me to his mouth for a passionate kiss. When he pulls back I'm dazed for a second.

"Chance." I grab his arm before he turns around. "I'm, well I um..... I just want you to know that ...." I take a deep breath. "I'm all in." I hope he knows what I mean when I look into his eyes with my heart on the line for him.

He leans back in and sweetly kisses my forehead. "You take my breath." One more soft kiss to my lips, and he's gone.

I drive the next four hours behind Chance until we arrive. We pull up to his house, and my bladder is demanding the bathroom.

He walks up to me beside my truck. "I need to check on Nana before I unpack. Lets leave the bags for now."

"I have to use the bathroom really bad, and I need a shower. You go ahead then I will come over afterwards."

"Sure honey, take my keys then when your done come to the diner. I will have us a late night meal ready."

"Good, I'm starving." I kiss him, grab my small bag, then practically run to the house.

I throw my bag down after grabbing shorts, and a t shirt for a quick shower. I finally release my bladder then step under the hot water in the shower. It feels so good on my sore muscles. I stay in as long as I can before I step out, and wrap a towel around myself.

I'm startled as the bathroom door flies open.

"Chance, there you ....."

I'm clutching my towel tight around my body staring at the crazy, rude bitch from the clothing store on my last visit to this town.

"Who the fuck are you? Oh my God, you're that fat cow from my store! What the hell are you doing in Chance's shower?" She is screaming at me like a banshee. "Where is Chance, does he know your in here? Never mind, I will wait for him in his bed just like before." She smirks at my ashen face.

I feel sick, this can't be happening. My mind is screaming at me to get out, to run like hell while I can. I hurriedly throw on my clothes, not bothering to dry off. My hair is a wet mess, and I'm shivering.

I grab my bag, not bothering to close it up. I'm in such a hurry that I don't realize I'm dropping stuff. I just need to get out. I throw my shit in my truck. I start sobbing, trying to catch my breath.

I can't drive like this, I need to calm down before I make myself sick. I grab my cell phone, and call Justine.

"Holy shit Carrie, its like two in the morning. Are you okay?" She sounds groggy, and I didn't even think of the time.

"I'm sorry, I just...." I feel my breath get stuck as a sob escapes me.

"Whats wrong? Talk to me Carrie." She is getting louder now.

"I think I made a mistake.... I can't think...."

"Take a deep breath, and listen to me honey. Breathe in." She takes a deep breath, and slowly releases it over and over till I follow along. "That's right, now slowly tell me you're okay."

"I'm okay. I... Oh man. I was confronted by a woman in his house."

"What?" She demands.

I explain everything from the moment I was startled by that crazy bitch. The more I talk the angrier I become.

"Did you ask him what the fuck she was doing in his bed?"

"No, I just lost my shit. This is why I need you. To calm my ass down, and think first. I love you my best friend. I need to go see him. I'm sorry I called so late. I will call you tomorrow." I can hear her calling my name as I hang up.

"Breathe Carrie." I take deep breaths to calm my anger down that's building up.

I get out of my truck, wipe my eyes, blow my nose, and head for the diner.

When I walk inside Chance is putting plates on the counter for us.

"There you are, I was beginning to wonder if you fell asleep." He stops and looks at my face. "Whats wrong?" He hurries around the counter, and pulls me into his arms.

I stiffen at his touch.

"Babe, whats wrong?"

"When is the last time you had a woman in your bed?" I feel nauseous just asking.

"What?"

"When!" I feel like a crazy woman out of control with my emotions. I can't stomach the idea that he had others while I was at home being miserable without him.

"Carrie, I haven't been with anyone other than you since the moment I saw you. I haven't cheated on you. Why would you ask me such a thing?" He seems hurt by my question.

"There is a woman in your bed right now!" I grit out. I pull myself from his arms. "I hear the truth in your words, but there is a woman in your bed." I wrap my arms around myself.

"I don't know what the hell is going on, but will you please look at me." He wraps his arms around me, and slowly turns me to face him. His hand pulls my eyes up to his. "Before I met you, I've had plenty of women." He holds my chin to ensure I stop trying to pull away. "I haven't been with anyone since the moment my eyes landed on you here in this diner with your ratty hair, grouchy attitude, and puffy eyes. I can't take back my past, but I need you to trust me okay?"

"Kiss me please." My lips tremble. I feel so raw, and vulnerable right now.

His lips take mine in what feels like desperation for me to believe him.

He leans his forehead on mine. "Lets get this shit settled." He pulls me by the hand out the door behind him. "I'm tired, hungry, and I fucking need to hold you."

He goes straight upstairs, and slams his bedroom door open.

"What the hell?" I mumble confused. There is no one there. The bed is perfectly made with no signs of anyone having been here.

"Who was it?" He asks.

"The woman from the clothing store. This doesn't make any sense, she said she was going back to your bed just like before."

"Honey, whatever the hell she is trying to pull, she has never been in my bed before." Chance grabs my hand.

"So, you know who I'm talking about?"

"Well, I'm not sure who your talking about, but it doesn't matter because I've never brought a woman home to my bed until you. This is my home. I just took females to the hotel."

"Well, she was here. The stuck up bitch. Ask Emily, she knows her name. She was running that clothing store Justine, and I went to when we were here last."

"Are you talking about Crystal?"

"I don't remember her name, but she was tall, blonde, stacked like a brick house." I sneer at him.

He starts fucking laughing. "Fake, stuck up bitch who treats people like shit. Yeah, that's Crystal."

"Well, she was here in your bed. Did you have a relationship with her before?" I turn to head down to the kitchen. I can't look at his bed right now.

"Why don't you make some coffee, I'll go get our food, and then we will talk."

I'm in the kitchen now, but I want to know. "Did you?" I can't stop myself from asking again.

"Shit" He takes a deep breath. "I fucked her once a few months ago. I never had a relationship with her. That's the truth." He turns and walks out the door.

I let go of the breath I was holding. I make coffee, and as I'm sitting down two cups he walks back in with our food.

"I'm sorry." I feel like I owe him that.

"I'm sorry she pulled that shit. Can we just talk about this shit tomorrow? Can we just eat, and go to bed. I'm.... Baby, please?" He kisses my shoulder from behind me.

I nod, sit down, and pick at my food. I eat a few bites, but my stomach just can't eat any more after all the turmoil.

"Come here." He scoots his chair back, and holds his hand out.

I straddle is lap, and just lay my head on his shoulder. I just need to be held, to feel wanted. We sit in silence for awhile, as he rubs my back.

"I'm going to go shower, why don't you get ready for bed so I can hold you more. Okay?"

"I think I'll use the other bathroom, take a few moments for myself."

He lifts me up, kisses me, and heads upstairs.

I brush my teeth, my hair, and take care of all the things I didn't before.

I step in the doorway of his bedroom, and he is finishing changing the sheets in his boxers.

"I thought it would make you feel better just in case."

"Thank you, that's sweet." I crawl in his bed feeling nervous for some reason.

"Relax babe." He slides in under the sheets, and pulls me to his chest. "Go to sleep."

I think I fell asleep the moment the words left his mouth.

I stretch feeling like I slept the sleep of the dead. I feel good, as I come in contact with a very hard body.

"Good morning." He pushes his hardness against my ass. "I was beginning to think you were never going to wake up. I'm so fucking hard for you." His teeth against my skin causes my body to shiver. "Take off your shorts Carrie."

"Oh God." I moan when his hand palms my breasts.

"Shorts."

I quickly push my shorts down and off.

"Put your leg back up over my thigh, and open yourself up to me. Let me inside of you." His fingers slide through my slit. "You're so fucking wet already for me." He rubs his cock through my wetness then shoves inside of me in one full thrust.

I cry out from the tightness, the fullness of him inside of me.

"This is going to be hard, and fast. Oh fuck babe, I can't get enough." His voice is deep and lust filled as his pace increases out of control. His fingers work my clit and the explosion of my release is incredible. I soak him causing him to holler out with his orgasm inside of me.

His breathing against my back is calming down. He slides out of me with a groan. "I wish I could stay inside of you all day." His lips travel down my shoulder, and arm. "I need to get over to the diner for my shift. I owe Emily, and Sonny for covering for me." He laughs but continues to nip at my skin.

"I need to find a job." I sigh.

"No hurry, take the day, and get to know the place first. If you come to the diner around five I will have a piece of peach pie for you, and then we can walk home together."

"Home, I like the sound of that." I kiss him before he scoots out of bed.

An hour later I drive around the town after exploring a little on foot and enjoying the sights. I decide to go the grocery store and grabs some ingredients for my homemade beef stew. Its about the only thing I can cook that's good. I want to surprise Chance.

I grab my bags, and head for my truck. When I try to start it nothing happens. "Shit, not now. Come on baby." I try again, and still nothing. I don't want to bother him at work by calling him. I'm a few miles from home so I don't have a choice but to grab my bags, and start walking.

I have meat so I know I need to hurry. I pick up my pace but after about twenty minutes I need to slow down just a little bit. I'm about halfway back when a truck pulls over.

"Need a ride?"

I look over to see a young man, maybe twenty five, smiling at me.

"Um, no thanks, but I appreciate the offer." I continue to walk.

"Carrie, right?" The truck slowly stays beside me.

"How do you know me?" I ask curiously.

"I work for Chance as his backup chef. I know you're Carrie because you're all he talked about, and he showed me a photo of you sleeping in his bed." He laughs.

"What?" I ask a little loudly.

"Shit, sorry." He stops his truck, and jumps out. "That came out wrong. It was a photo of just your hair, and face. You were sleeping peacefully. I made a stupid joke about him getting in your pants, and he almost ripped my head off. My God, where are my manners. I'm Sonny." He grabs a bag out of my arms, and shakes my hand. "I've never seen him so gone for someone. Call him, he will tell you to let me give you a ride. Come on." He grabs the other bag from me. " Why would you walk this far to get groceries? Its to far to carry this shit."

"I didn't walk, but my truck broke down at the grocery store. I don't want to bother him while he's working." I still feel a little uneasy, but he seems like a nice guy.

"If I leave you here to walk, and Chance finds out, I'll not only get fired, but he will kick my ass. Take pity on me, please!" His smile, and pout on his lip makes me give in.

"Okay, okay, I give." I laugh.

"Yes!" He throws his arm around me, and leads me to his truck. "Your chariot awaits." He opens my door and helps me in.

"Thanks Sonny."

"See, that wasn't so bad."

"You're very charming, and I do remember Chance mentioning you this morning." I relax back against the seat.

"You can drop your groceries off then I will take you back to your truck. I'm good with engines too."

"I wouldn't want to trouble you, I can get Chance to fix it when he gets off work."

"Are you kidding me, and miss the opportunity to tease him about rescuing his girl. No way!" His laughter is contagious.

"I'm not a girl, and thank you. I will be in your debt." I laugh with him.

"A good home cooked meal would be nice." He peeks into my grocery bags.

"Beef stew, nothing special, but your welcome to join us. Come over around six." I gather up my bags to head inside when Sonny grabs them from me.

"Let me."

"Thanks."

The groceries get put away then we head back for my truck.

While he is looking under the hood of my truck he engages me in conversation.

"So, Carrie, how did my buddy Chance get so lucky in catching your eye?"

"I helped his Nana get back to his Grandpa. She wondered off and wound up knocking on my hotel room in the middle of the night. Grandpa offered me a free meal at the diner for my help."

"Were you all decked out, and stole his heart?" He laughs when he shuts the hood.

"No, my hair was a rats nest, my makeup was non existent, and I hadn't had my coffee yet so I was grouchy as hell. He probably thought I looked scary." I couldn't help but laugh which caused me to snort once.

"Start it up." He smiles at my face turning red.

"Thank you Sonny." It starts, and purrs like a kitten.

"Anytime doll face." He winks as he pulls away in his truck.

My cellphone rings. "Hello."

"Hey babe, I just wanted to hear your voice. I'm on a little break. Did you get some exploring done?" Chance's voice brings a huge smile to my face.

"I miss you too."

"Is it that obvious?" I can hear the smile in his voice.

"I'm going to cook us supper tonight."

"Uh, Carrie..."

"Stop it, I do know how to cook one good homemade meal. Asshole." I can't help but laugh at his worry over eating my cooking. He knows I can't cook. "Listen, I invited your friend Sonny over to eat with us. I hope that's okay? I guess I should have mentioned it first."

"You met Sonny?"

"Yeah, my truck broke down at the store, and I had to walk. He saw me, and was kind enough to give me a ride and fix my truck."

"Why didn't you call me? Dammit Carrie, I would have came and got you. You didn't need to walk." His voice is a little loud.

I don't say anything because I know he is worried and he doesn't mean to yell, but my heart hurts instantly from his tone.

"Carrie?"

"I'm sorry, I need to go. Its going to take awhile for the stew to cook, so I will see you when you get home." I hang up feeling sick to my stomach. I know this relationship is new, but his tone brought back too many memories.

My cell begins to ring again, but I just can't answer it right now. I turn it off, and lean my head onto the steering wheel. I breath deep to calm my nerves.

I know Chance is no where near the man my ex was. I just need to sort myself out because my heart hurts right now.

I go to put the truck in gear when I notice an envelope on the seat. I open it and there is a picture of Chance with his hand on some woman's ass. It looks like he is at the bar. Why the hell is this in my truck? Is this an old photo or a new one? The woman has her back to the camera, but she is young, and has the body of a model. I look at it a moment longer before I throw it down, and head for home.

When I pull up Chance is pacing back, and forth with his hands in his hair. When he sees me he runs up to my truck. I no sooner turn the truck off then he has my door open.

"Carrie." His eyes look frantic as he undoes my seat belt to pull me into his arms. "Babe, I was worried, I didn't.... I thought you left me." His voice sounds gruff.

"I'm sorry I hung up on you. I know you were just worried, and I freaked out about your tone." I lean into his embrace to breath in his scent. He smells like man, and food. Its comforting. "I would never leave without telling you I was. I'm a lot stronger than I use to be. I will never be treated badly again, by anyone. I know that's not you, but I needed a moment to get my head on straight."

"Carrie."

"Shhh" I put my fingers on his lips. "When you raised your voice to me out of fear, and I know it was out of fear, my heart hurt." A small sob escaped my lips.

"Don't you know that I love you baby? I love you." His lips are so gentle against mine.

"Chance, I ...."

"Shhh, its okay." He kisses me again. "I need to get back to work, I have a few more hours left. Are you going to come over at five for pie?"

"Yeah, I wouldn't pass up pie." I smile, feeling lighter.

"Sonny fixed your truck?"

"Yes, something about my coil wire being off. Whatever that means."

"That's weird, okay, as long as its fixed."

"See you at five."

I get the stew on the stove then get myself a fresh shower. I pull on a sundress with a sweater.

I enter the busy diner at four fifty five. I see Emily and she waves me over to a table in a corner booth.

"Hey Carrie, how are you? I was hoping I would get to see you soon, I missed you." She hugs me tight.

She is so sweet, I feel like I've known her forever.

"Uncle Chance is backed up with orders, so it could be a little while before he is free."

"That's okay, I'll wait."

"Coffee?"

"Yes please, and Chance promised me pie."

"Coming right up."

I look around at the busy diner and notice a lot of people finishing up their dinner. It seems to be slowing down but everyone is talking, and it feels like a nice place to be.

Emily brings me my coffee, and pie then rushes around picking up dirty dishes, and refilling cups.

I sit back and enjoy my pie while waiting for Chance.

Ten minutes later that Crystal bitch comes in, and heads behind the counter toward the kitchen I feel my fist clenching.

When the diner is down to a few people and it gets to be five thirty I'm still clenching my fist because that bitch is still back in the kitchen.

I get up and head for the restroom to calm myself down because I'm getting more pissed.

I'm washing my face with cold water when she enters behind me.

"Oh hey, Connie right?"

"Carrie." I grit out as I dry my hands and face trying to ignore her.

"I need to repair my lipstick." She smirks at me in the mirror.

I know she is trying to get under my skin so I just walk out.

I see Chance coming out of the kitchen looking pissed off. "I don't care, I want her banned. No one is allowed in my kitchen unless I invite them in."

"I didn't see her or trust me she wouldn't have made it back there." Emily tells Chance as she follows him.

"Hey babe, I'm sorry I'm late. Its been crazy busy." He leans in to kiss me as I turn my head away. "What?" He seems confused.

I reach over, and grab a napkin to dip in a glass of water left on the counter. I reach up to wipe his mouth, and cheek. I throw the napkin down. I'm fuming inside because I know she did that shit on purpose, but to see that lipstick on his mouth turns my guts.

"Fucking Crystal, I swear babe she cornered me in the kitchen, tried to kiss me. I pushed her off. I didn't know that shit was on my face."

"I know, I believe you, I just......" I turn around and walk outside.

"Carrie!" Chance grabs my hand. "She started arguing about me taking her out. I told her no, that I'm in a relationship. I had my hands full of dirty pans, and she grabbed my face. I couldn't stop her fast enough. I'm sorry, I didn't even know she was even in there at first till Henry said something. Henry is another cook." He is talking so fast.

"Shut up Chance!" I grab his face and slam my mouth on his. I want to erase that bitch from my man. I feel angry, and like a savage. I grab his hair and pull his mouth firmer against mine.

"Fuck babe!" He is trying to catch his breath when I pull my mouth off. "Oh hell yes!"

I squeal as he throws me over his shoulder, smacks my ass hard, and practically runs toward home.

"My dress! Chance, put me down." I suck in my breath when his hand connects with my ass again.

He fucking growls at me when he slams the door shut behind us. He has me thrown down on the couch in seconds. "Damn, your beautiful." His hand runs up my inner thigh when he comes down on top of me. His mouth is hot, and demanding when his fingers slide into the edge of my panties. "I want to...."

Someone knocks on the door loudly.

"Shit, its Sonny. I forgot he was coming over." I laugh as he groans into my neck.

"Maybe he will go away." His fingers barely skim across my wetness when the knocking starts again.

"You'll survive till later." I giggle as he gives me the death stare.

He stands up and stares at me while he licks his finger tips with my juices on them. "Come on." He pulls me up then straightens my dress.

"Your hard." I skim my nails across his bulge before I push him toward the door.

"Minx." He smacks my ass.

Chance

I have to adjust myself before I open the door. "Sonny, hey man. Come on in." I shake his hand.

"Am I interrupting?" He laughs at me, then I notice Carrie is fixing her hair behind me.

"Yes"

"Chance!" Carrie pinches my butt behind me. "Come on in Sonny. He's just teasing."

"I don't think so." Sonny mumbles under his breath.

"Thanks for helping Carrie out today man. I owe you one."

"No you don't, Carrie does. That's why I'm here for her homemade beef stew." He smells the air.

I was so wrapped up in her that I didn't even notice the wonderful smell. My stomach growls.

"Come on into the kitchen guys. The stew should be ready, and I have some fresh baked bread on the table."

"You made fresh baked bread too, man I'm in love." Sonny smiles as he grabs bowls out of the cupboard.

"I bought bread at the deli, I'm not that talented." She sits down beside me at the table as I serve her.

"I could have got it, but thank you."

"Babe, let me take care of you." I say softly in her ear while putting bread on her plate. I love seeing the blush run up her neck.

"So, Sonny, how long have you known Chance?" Carrie asks.

"We met about seven years ago in the Marines. I was an eighteen year old cocky fucker, and Chance helped me get through two years of fucked up shit before I got out. I had nowhere to go, so he brought me here, and I cook for him."

"Where did you learn how to cook?"

Carrie doesn't notice Sonny's face of unease.

"My Gamma taught me before she died."

"Aw, that's sweet. I'm sure you do her proud."

"I try." He continues to shovel his face full of food with his head down.

"Has she been gone long?"

"Carrie." I try to get her attention.

"No, its okay." Sonny clears his throat. "She was murdered while I was in the Marines. A home invasion gone wrong."

"Oh God, I'm so sorry Sonny." Carrie leans forward, and grabs Sonny's hands in comfort.

"Thank you, I haven't spoken about it in awhile, but you are right about my cooking. I try to do her proud every time I make a plate." He smiles as Carrie sits back down.

"Maybe sometime you can cook for Chance and I, maybe make her favorite dish in her honor."

"That sounds great." Sonny relaxes.

"Does anyone want coffee, or a beer?" Carrie stands up to clear the table.

"Sit down Carrie, we got this. You cooked for us, so let us clean up." Sonny grabs her bowl out of her hand.

Carrie is standing, and staring at us like we have two heads.

"Babe, take this beer, go sit down to relax, and take it easy." I kiss her, and push her toward the living room.

I watch from the sink of dishes till I see her sit down on the couch before I turn to Sonny. "Are you okay?" I hand him a bowl to rinse.

"Yeah, I haven't spoken about what happened to Gamma to anyone in a long time. That woman of yours is something else." He stares back toward the living room with an odd look on his face.

"I've never met anyone like her. She is an amazing person." I smile at Sonny as we finish up the dishes.

"I was happy to help her out man. I owe you my life, so helping a beautiful woman out for you is no problem." He laughs at me over the sound of my growling.

"I'm throwing in a movie." Carrie hollers.

"Shit, no chick flicks man." Sonny mumbles as we enter the living room.

"Chick flicks! Hey, for that I should take out my first choice, and put in Letters to Juliet just for you Sonny." She stands back up from the DVD player laughing.

I slap Sonny on the back of his head for staring at her ass. "What did you put in honey?" I smirk at Sonny's face of surprise that he was caught.

"The Fast and the Furious. I hope you two don't mind, but Vin Diesel is hot!"

"Hey!" I grab her ass to pull her down beside me.

"Oh shit, did I say that last part out loud. I meant to say that I love the fast cars." Her laughter is sweet.

"Smart ass."

We spend the next couple of hours watching movies, eating popcorn, and laughing with a few more beers.

"Do you care if I crash on your couch. I've had a few too many beers to drive." Sonny quietly asks.

"She already took your keys man when she was throwing popcorn at you earlier." I laugh as he taps his pockets.

"Thanks Carrie." Sonny slurs just a little bit.

"No problem, I'll grab an extra blanket, and pillow for you." Carrie leaves the room.

"Help yourself to the fridge, or whatever you need man." I yawn as I stand up.

"Thanks man."

"I got those Carrie." I take the blanket, and pillow to Sonny before I head to bed.

I step in the bedroom just as I see Carrie grabbing a nightgown. "No." I take it and throw it back on the dresser.

She smiles, and lifts her arms while I pull her dress over her head. "Holy shit." I feel my breath rush out when my eyes travel down her body. She is in a skimpy black bra, and underwear set.

"You like it?" She twirls around.

"That's sexy as hell, but it needs to go." I kiss down her neck, nipping with my teeth while my fingers undo her bra strap. I slowly slide the straps down her arms to reveal her breasts. They are more than a handful. I lean down, and suck a plump nipple into my mouth.

Her head leans back releasing a moan from her throat.

"Lay down on the bed." I stalk her as her body lays out for me. I bend down and lick up her stomach. "Lift your ass." I use my teeth to pull her underwear down her thighs, letting my nose skim across her slit, breathing in her smell.

"Oh fuck." Her hips push up at me.

"Spread yourself open for for. That's right, now slide your fingers through your pussy.

"Chance."

"Let me see how wet you are for me."

She lifts her fingers for my inspection. I suck her juices off her fingers onto my tongue. She is very wet.

"Tell me what you want right now." I stare into her lust filled eyes. Her breath is coming faster.

"No foreplay, just fuck me hard. I need you."

Those are the hottest fucking words I have ever heard out of her mouth. I strip in seconds, and posed above her.

"Take my cock inside you baby." I groan when her warm hand wraps around me. I'm so fucking hard.

She lines me up. "Fuck me." I slam inside of her so fast and full.

"Oh God yes!" She screams.

I pull my hips back, and slam home inside of her again.

"More dammit!"

"Make yourself cum on my cock, and I'll fuck you so hard you won't be able to fucking walk right tomorrow." I slam hard again.

Her fingers begin working her clit into a frenzy until I feel her hot juices explode onto me.

"Hold on to the bed!" I barely wait for her hand to grip the headboard before I slam over and over like an animal inside of her. I feel my balls tighten up before I holler out my release.

I'm so exhausted, I collapse onto her before I roll to put her onto my chest. I remember mumbling about her being my world then I was out.

I blink from the light in my eyes. I roll over to reach for Carrie, but the bed is empty.

"Babe." I groan . I stumble out of bed to the toilet then take a quick shower. I throw on some sweatpants then head downstairs.

I smell coffee, and bacon in the air. Sonny is setting at the table eating.

"Morning boss." Sonny laughs when I flip him off.

"Knock that boss shit off asshole." I pour myself coffee.

"I made plenty. I figured I could cook to say thanks for the evening of company last night."

"No thanks needed man, that's what friends are for."

"You better tell princess to get her lazy ass out of bed, and eat before I eat it all." Sonny sets his cup down.

"She isn't in bed. You haven't seen her?" I grab my cell off the table.

"I've been awake for an hour man. I haven't seen her." Sonny sees my worried expression as I wait for her to answer her phone.

"It goes straight to voice mail." I head for the front door to go find her.

"I'm coming too." Sonny catches up.

I get outside, and her truck door is wide open, but she is nowhere in sight. "Carrie!" I yell to see if she is anywhere near.

"Her truck is here, so she has to be near. Maybe she's at the diner."

"Chance, wait!" Sonny is leaning in her truck. "You need to see this." He turns around and hands me a photo.

"Why in the fuck is this in her truck? This looks like one of my drunken nights at the bar , but this is an old photo. Maybe two years ago. That's the girl you hooked me up with over that pool game." I'm confused.

"That's weird, you didn't even know her then. Why the fuck would she have this in her truck?"

"Lets find her." I take off toward the diner feeling sick. First Crystals bullshit now this.

I walk in to Emily laughing with a customer. "Em, you seen Carrie?" I pull her to the side.

"Yeah, she was here about an hour or more ago. She got some breakfast for Nana, and Grandpa. She said she hadn't had a chance to see them yet,and she wanted to check on them. She said you needed some rest so she took what I had prepared."

"Thanks Em."

"Are you okay?" Her brow is drawn down.

I realize I must looked worried. "Yeah, I just wanted her to have breakfast. Sorry Em, but I'll talk to you later."

"I'll catch up to you in a minute." Sonny is staring at Em.

"Sure man." I take off.

My Grandpa is sitting behind the desk when I walk in.

"Hey Chance, I'm glad you came to see me." Grandpa hugs me. "You hungry? That girl of yours brought plenty. She sure is a sweetheart."

"Yes she is, thanks Grandpa. Is she with Nana?" I head on back to Nana's room before he has a chance to answer.

I stand at the doorway where Carrie has her back to me. She is feeding Nana.

"Did you see my John, isn't he handsome?"

"I sure did see him, he couldn't keep his eyes off you. You're a lucky lady."

"He says I'm his girl. He makes me so happy." Nana claps her hands together as if she is a teenager again. "We're going to go to the movies, but Pa says Jon better behave." She leans toward Carrie. "Hopefully he doesn't behave to well." She laughs.

"You hoping for him to sneak a kiss, you sly girl you." Carrie laughs quietly.

"I'm so tired Emily, can you sit with me till I fall asleep." Nana lays her head back.

I feel the smile fade from my face. The sadness that Dementia can still her memories from moment to the next. My Nana is my world.

"Sure Nana, you rest easy now." Carrie leans up, and kisses her on the forehead while Nana holds her hand.

My heart squeezes in my chest. I turn to Grandpa watching me. He motions for me to follow him.

We step back into the lobby where Sonny is waiting.

"She's okay, she is with Nana."

"Okay, I'm going back over to the diner. I will see you in a bit." Sonny leaves after checking on Carrie.

"That's quite a woman you got there son."

"Yes." I sit down, and look over at Grandpa. "She's the one."

"I know." He smiles in understanding.

We sit in silence until Carrie walks back in with tears in her eyes. She walks straight to Grandpa's arms.

"You sweet, sweet girl."

"Thank you for letting me spend time with her." She kisses his cheek then walks over to me.

"You okay?" I put my arms around her.

"I am now." She lays her head on my chest.

"I called your cell because I couldn't find you when I woke up." I soothe my hand down her hair.

"I'm sorry I worried you, but my cell didn't ring." She pulls her cell out to show me only to realize it is dead. "Shit."

"Your truck door was wide open."

"Huh?" She pulls back confused then notices the photo in my hand. "Why do you have that?"

"I was going to ask you the same thing?"

"I found it on the seat of my truck yesterday after I got out of the grocery store. I forgot about it after that shit at the diner yesterday. I was going to mention it." She shrugs her shoulders.

"Its an old photo, maybe two years ago."

"I know."

"You do?" I feel the tension leave me.

"Well yeah. Look at it closer. I was pissed at first till I thought about it. I threw it down to discuss later, but got distracted by that bit..... I mean woman." Her neck flushes red when she remembers my Grandpa standing there.

I can hear him chuckling as he leaves the lobby.

"Did you enjoy talking to my Nana?" I kiss her forehead to breath in her scent. She always smells like peaches, like her body lotion.

"She's wonderful." She wraps her arms around my neck. "I really like her." I can hear the sadness in her voice.

"I know honey. Lets go home." I grab her hand, and head out.

"Hey breakfast! Yum." Carrie digs right in. "Where's Sonny?" She asks with a mouthful of bacon. "Mmmm."

"He cooked us breakfast then went over to the diner." I sit down beside her to watch her eat.

"What?" She covers her full mouth.

"I love having you here." I get lost in her eyes.

"I..."

"I love you." I kiss her cheek. "I'm heading over to the diner for my shift. You enjoy your day." I pull my t shirt on that I left lay. When I turn around Carrie jumps at me.

I grab her ass to hold her to me. "Hey."

"You can't leave with a little kiss like that to hold me over." She takes mouth sweetly at first, then when she opens wider, I take control of the kiss with my tongue.

When I pull my mouth back she is breathing harder. I slide her down the front of my body then leave out the front door.

I walk slow so my cock goes down. I'm hard all the time around her, and my smile is big.

The next several hours fly by. Sonny and I cook breakfast, prep for lunch, and prep for dinner. Sonny and I decide to take a break outback.

"She tell you why she had that photo?" Sonny lights up a cigarette.

"She said someone put it in her truck while she was at the grocery store. I thought you quit?" I nod toward the cigarette.

He throws it down, and stomps on it. "I did, I just... Fuck I don't know!" He rakes his hands through his hair. "Ever since my Gamma's name came up I've been a little frazzled. I miss her so much."

"I'm sorry I caused you any kind of pain." Carrie quietly says when she walks up to us in the back alley.

"You Darlin', have nothing to be sorry about." Sonny pulls her into a hug. "I'm the one who should be sorry. I'm sorry that I don't speak of her more often. She deserves that from me. Its just been rough."

"Anytime you want to go down memory lane you come see me. I'm a pretty good listener." Carrie comes into my arms.

"I appreciate that, I will sometime. Thank you." Sonny heads back inside.

"Give me those lips." I pull her chin up, and kiss her properly.

"Okay, I need to go so you can finish up. Come home to me."

"I love that. Coming home to you." I kiss her one more time.

Emily is busy getting the food out that Sonny and I have ready for the customers. She is working at a fast pace.

"Slow down Em, your going to run out of steam." I laugh as she sticks her tongue out at me like when she was little.

"This is my last table, and my feet are killing me. Henry should be here soon so you two can leave also."

"You got plans tonight Emily?" Sonny asks when she returns to the kitchen.

"Nope, I'm going to just put my feet up, and read a book for awhile." She hangs up her apron, and grabs her purse to leave.

"Can you take this to Nana and Grandpa on your way?" I hand her a bag for their supper.

"Sure, you going to stop over later?"

"Always do."

"Love you."

"Love you too." Emily hurry's out the door.

"She seemed to be in a rush." Sonny watches her.

"I think she has a date." Sonny seems taken back by my statement. "I heard her on the phone talking about some guy. Something about finally making the stubborn jackass notice her. I don't know."

Henry comes walking in as I have my back to them.

"Son of a bitch." Sonny is mumbling on his way out.

"Your messing with that jackass again." Henry is laughing.

"Its so easy, especially when it comes to Em." Smirking, I turn to head home.

I'm about to walk in my door when my cell rings. "Whats up Sonny?" I smile to myself.

"Your an asshole! Do you know that, you fucker." He is laughing.

"You ran straight to her place didn't you?" I laugh even harder.

"She said I was an idiot for listening to you. Thanks a lot asshole."

"You deserved it man. Why don't you just ask her out man? Don't give me the bullshit about being a few years older than her either, or any other crappy excuse."

"I just wanted to call you an asshole man." He hangs up on me just as he comes up behind me.

"Hey!" I punch his arm as he follows me into the house.

When I enter the kitchen I am stunned by her beauty. She is wearing one of my long shirts, her hair is a mess, and she looks like she just crawled out of bed.

"I fell asleep earlier. I need some coffee." Carrie mumbles.

She reaches up to grab a coffee cup, and my shirt rises up revealing a bare ass cheek.

"Holy shit." Sonny says as he walks into my back.

The coffee cup crashes to the floor when Carrie whips around startled.

The front of the shirt is unbuttoned halfway down.She quickly clutches it tight in her fist.

"Don't move baby." I hurry over, and lift her out of the mess.

"I'll get the broom." Sonny hurry's to clean up the mess.

"I need pants." Carrie runs out of the kitchen.

"That was entertaining."

"Shut up asshole." I laugh quietly to Sonny.

I get Carrie a new cup, and fill it for her just how she like it with creamer when she comes back into the kitchen.

"Did you bring me flowers? Your so sweet Chance." She inhales the flowers. "They kind of stink." She laughs.

"I didn't." I take the flowers from her and give her the coffee.

"Well somebody did. They weren't here when I laid down. Maybe Emily did it."

"She was with Sonny and I all day." I turn to Sonny.

Sonny pulls out his cell. I can see his jaw ticking with anger. He turns his back to us. "I'm coming over." He walks out the front door.

"Has anything else odd happened that you can remember?" I sit her down at the kitchen table with me.

"Just the photo." She drinks her coffee.

"Don't forget about your truck." I stare at the flowers.

"My truck, but I thought....." She grabs her stomach then runs out of the room.

"Carrie?" I jump up and reach her just as she vomits in the toilet. I pull her hair back from her face.

"I think I'm okay." She stands up.

I run a cold washcloth across her face and neck to help her feel better. I grab a hair tie and put her long hair in it. "Baby, you should...."

"Oh God....." She bends down. "My stomach hurts really bad." She curls up in a ball on the floor.

I kneel down to her and she is sweating, and shaking. "Carrie." I pull out my cell and call an ambulance when she begins to dry heave.

The ambulance wouldn't allow me to ride along, and by the time I got to the hospital she was already behind closed doors.

They can't answer any questions yet, the doctor will be out soon, just take a seat. All the things they keep telling me isn't helping the fear churning in my gut.

Sonny and Em are trying to keep me calm as I pace. I need fucking answers.

"They can at least tell me if shes okay dammit!" I continue to pace and watch the doors.

Finally the doctor approaches me. "Are you Chance?"

"Hows Carrie? Can I see her?"

"Shes doing much better, but can you tell me how she might have ingested pesticide?"

"What?" I'm stunned at his words. "What the hell are you talking about?"

"She had high levels of pesticide poisoning in her stomach lining. We had to pump her stomach to get the levels down. We will be keeping her overnight for precautions and to be sure her system is cleared."

"Can I see her?" I need to see her for myself.

"Shes been asking for you. Follow me."

We all three follow behind the doctor. "You have company."

I walk in to see her curled up on her side looking very pale. I'm by her side in seconds. I brush back her hair that has come loose from her ponytail. I kiss her forehead. "I'm here baby."

"Chance, I'm a mess." She tries to smile. "Can I get a shower?"

"Let me get her a nurse." The doctor says.

"No, I don't need a nurse." Carrie squeezes my hand.

"I'll help her doc, thank you."

"We brought you some clean clothes Carrie." Emily sets down a bag.

"Thank you." She sets up and leans her head on my shoulder.

"Okay?" I run my hand down her back.

"I feel weak, like I lost all my energy. Fucking pesticide poisoning. How the fuck did that happen? Someone had to have been in the house when I was sleeping. I was fine before I laid down to take a nap. You said you didn't bring the flowers, but I didn't consume them just smelled them. The only thing I had after waking up was the coffee you made."

"Wait, I didn't make that coffee. I had just arrived when you came into the kitchen. I thought you had made it earlier since it was almost empty."

"No, I literally just crawled out of bed. I didn't even know you were there until Sonny spoke. I was still half asleep." She blushes, remembering her state of dress.

"Why was you sleeping so late in the day? We're you sick before?" Sonny asks.

"No, I was reading in bed. I was waiting on Chance to come home.That's why I was in just your shirt." She looks at me. "I wanted to surprise you." She says quietly. " I guess I dozed off, but it couldn't have been more than an hour."

"Come on, let me help you shower then we can visit more. I want you comfortable." I lift her into my arms.

"Chance." She grabs her gown to stop from flashing Sonny and Emily.

I help her strip the gown, and sit her on the toilet seat so I can adjust the water temperature.

"Can you move that chair into the shower stall that way I don't get dizzy?"

I just stare at her when I begin to strip.

"What are you doing?" She laughs.

"I'm helping you."

"I can do it myself if I just have the chair."

I ignore her as I finish taking all my clothes off. I do grab the chair and put it in the shower before I pick her up. I sit down, and hold her in my lap.

"Let me take care of you. I need too." I wrap myself around her and lay my head on her shoulder with my face buried in her neck.

I feel her fingers run through my hair before I lean her head back into the water. I shampoo her hair and slowly cleanse her body, loving her as I do. I needed to reassure myself that she is okay and here with me.

"Okay, your all clean."

"My turn." She grabs the shampoo and works her fingers into my scalp. "Let me." She begins rubbing herself back and forth on my lap, as her fingers rub soap across my body.

"Carrie, you need to stop baby. I want to take care of you." I can't stop my cock from being hard as a rock when I'm near her.

"You are taking care of me." She strokes me then leans up and slides down onto me.

I hold her by the hips as soap runs down between us. "Fuck." I moan. "Hold still, let me make you feel good." I lift her up and down onto me. Her teeth scrape across my neck, and I can hear all her pleasured moans in my ear.

"Fuck me, make me feel it. I want to feel all of you." She bites me hard in the neck.

"Minx." I growl. I pull her body up, and turn her facing away from me where the water sprays onto her clit."Touch yourself."

Her hand is stroking her clit before I can finish the words. I push hard up inside of her. I reach my hands down and spread her pussy wide open to the spray.

"Fuck yes." She begins bucking harder as I push up into her hard. "I'm can't stop, oh God....I...."

I cover her mouth with mine as she screams her release into my mouth. I pump my cum up inside of her. I can feel each throb as if its a heartbeat. My fingers work her clit until she begs me to stop. Only after she floods my fingers do I stop.

"I can't move." She is sprawled wide open on my lap facing the water to worn out to move.

"You're so fucking beautiful just like this, full of me and worn out." I nip her skin as I grab the wash rag again. "I love you."

I begin to wash her all over again starting with her luscious breasts.

Twenty minutes later we are dressed, and she is back in her bed.

"My daughter and family are coming here this weekend. Sonny, do you think you could help me with the cooking for a get together?"

"Babe, we don't need a big deal. Your still here in the hospital, and your thinking about others. Its only four days away." I hesitate to ask. "Do you want me to call Alexa?"

"No!" She grabs my arm. "Please, she will freak out, and be here in a few hours."

"Okay, but when she gets here, you need to let her know so she doesn't find out on her own." I rub her hand to ease her nerves.

"We could close the diner for the day and just have a relaxing get together. Easy and simple." Sonny suggests.

"Will you make some of your Gamma's dishes?" Carrie pleads.

"For you sweetheart, anything." Sonny winks at her.

"Stop hitting on my woman, you ass." I laugh because Sonny just can't help himself.

"I'll hold you to-that." Carrie winks right back.

"Stop encouraging him. His ego is big enough." Emily smiles.

"That's not all that's big." He wiggles his eyebrows at Emily.

I see her face flush as she turns to look out the window.

"I need some coffee, Come on Sonny."

I kiss Carrie. "I'll grab you a juice and a muffin."

"I would appreciate the juice, but hold off on the muffin." She rubs her stomach.

"Can I get a kiss too Emily?" Sonny mumbles.

"Sonny." I hiss under my breath.

"You be sure about that big guy, because one of these days I'm going to surprise you. I'm not sure you really could handle me." Emily winks at his stunned face, and then turns her back to him.

"Come on big guy." I'm still laughing as I push him out the door.

Carrie

"Are you okay Emily?" I seen her back stiffen after she turned around. I saw a flash of hurt.

"Yeah, sure." She shrugs her shoulders.

"Turn around." I hold my hand out.

She turns around, and I can see the shine of her tears in her eyes as she grabs my hand.

"Shh, its okay." I pull her into my arms as if she were my own child.

"I'm such a fool." She cries quietly in my arms.

"Its not foolish to love someone." I gently soothe her by running my hand through her hair.

"It is when he has a reputation for being with a lot of women. I can't compete with them. I don't want to compete with them." She sits up and wipes her face. "I'm not cut out for one night stands."

"Ah sweety, have you ever told him how you feel?"

"I don't need too, its always right here for everyone to see." She points at her face.

"Maybe, but some men can be dense sometimes honey."

"Hey!" Chance loses his smile as he sees Emily's face. "I heard that." He hands me my juice and a muffin.

"Thanks but I don't think I can eat."

"Maybe later." He kisses my lips.

"I think I'm going to go home to get some rest. I'm glad your going to be okay Carrie." She hugs me.

"Chance, can you drive Emily home?"

"I'll take her." Sonny steps forward with his coffee.

Emily's face starts to panic showing her vulnerability right now.

"Let Chance take her. I have ulterior motives to you staying here for a little while longer." I rub my hands together. "We're going to talk menu's for the get together."

Sonny looks a little confused at my suggestion. I look to Chance for understanding.

"I need to talk to Emily anyway. Come on girl, let me take you home."

Emily nods with relief.

"I'll be right back honey." Chance kisses me, and feeling his hand on my cheek lets me feel his love. "Sonny, you don't leave this room until I return." He stands up and looks back at me. "You're my world."

He man hugs Sonny while staring at me.

"Semper Fi."

The door no sooner shuts then my smile fades.

"You just wanted to have me all to yourself didn't ya Darlin'?" Sonny laughs while sitting on the end of my bed.

I cross my arms, just staring at him until he realizes I'm upset.

"What?" His smile falls away. "I'm just teasing you."

"Talk to me about Emily?" I continue to mean mug him.

"Shit, Carrie." He stands up, and runs his hands through his hair. "You sound like Chance." He sits down with his elbows on his knees.

I patiently continue to stare at him.

"What do you want from me?" He seems frustrated. "I have a lot of baggage that I don't want to taint her." He wipes his face then looks at me.

"You're hurting her." I grab his hand. "She is a strong woman, but by shutting her out on the real you, you are hurting her."

"That's the last thing I want. I know she loves me. Her eyes tell me so every time I'm near her. Our friendship is complicated, okay." He turns his eyes away. "Shit, she was crying over me again."

"Do you want some advice from a woman."

"Can't hurt." He smiles sadly.

"Stop with the bullshit, man up, and tell her how you really feel. Fears and all Sonny. She needs that from you.She needs your trust." I stare at him until his eyes meet mine.

"Damn, your harsh." Sonny nods his head.

"Just being honest."

"Thanks Carrie. Chance is one lucky son of a bitch." He leans over and kisses my cheek.

"Yes I am." Chance comes in smiling. "Did you get your menu under control?" He sits by my hip.

"Gamma's lasagna, garlic bread, and blackberry cobbler." Sonny winks at me.

"Damn, my mouths watering already." Chance leans in and nuzzles my neck.

"I'm going to head out, maybe go get some sleep."

"Take care driving home Sonny." I wave.

"Thanks for the advice, and maybe take some of that for yourself." Sonny blows me a kiss.

"Asshole." Chance throws a pillow at his retreating back.

"Did Emily get home okay?"

"Yeah, but she was so quiet, and I'm worried about her. Sonny needs to get his head out of his ass."

"He loves her." I say softly.

"I know, he just needs to believe in himself more."

"I want to thank you." I touch his face.

"Hey, what's going on with you?" He leas his forehead to mine.

I see so much love in his eyes. Its an overwhelming feeling to know that someone truly loves you just the way you are.

"Thank you for being patient with me. Through all my fears, and insecurities. For loving me." I put my hand behind his neck, and pull his mouth to mine. I pour all my love into the kiss.

"I love you." Chance whispers against my lips.

"I love you too." I let the words out. Finally letting go of the fear of rejection, of not being enough.

"Finally." He chuckles, sliding in beside me to hold me in his arms.

"Hey!" I smack his arm.

"I know you love me baby, your face tells me everyday. Its nice to hear the words though."

We cuddle up, exhausted, and fall asleep in each others arms.

I get released the next day. We arrive home around ten in the morning.

When I enter the kitchen I notice the coffee pot, and my mug are gone.

"The officer took them to check for fingerprints. They said it was unlikely. but they still had to check."

"Okay." I feel a little uneasy being back here.

"I'm going to grab a quick shower then we can head over to the diner before the lunch crowd comes in." Chance kisses me then heads to the shower.

I grab the stack of mail on the kitchen table that Chance grabbed on the way in. "Junk, junk, bills, more junk..... What is this?" A plain envelope with nothing on it but my name.

I open it to discover a bunch of photos. More photos of Chance with other women at the bar. I skim through quite a few before my breath leaves me on the last one. Its a photo of myself in the shower. The photo was taken from inside our bedroom looking into the bathroom. I'm leaning my head back smiling, looking happy.

This is a violation of my privacy. The more I stare at the photo, the more pissed I get. Some mother fucker was seeing me at a moment where no one but myself, or Chance should have seen.

"Babe, have you seen my..... Hey, what's wrong? What the fuck!" Chance walks up to the photos all over the table where I dropped them. "Where the fuck did these come from?"

"The mail." I'm crumbling the photo in my fist.

"Someone is fucking pissing....."

"Did you know these photos were out there?" I have to ask.

"No, but they are all in the bar where everyone has a phone. Babe, I can't change my past." He cups my cheek. "Hey."

I'm so angry I can't stop from clenching my jaw.

"Carrie?" He looks down to the crinkling noise in my hand. "Let me see." He grabs my hand, waiting for me to release the photo.

I release the photo, and I can see the moment it registers to him what the photo is. His face becomes instantly enraged. "That's from our room." He crushes the photo, and pulls me against his chest. He continues to hold me until my body finally relaxes against his chest.

I know I feel tears coming on.

"I'm going to walk you to Nana, and Grandpas for awhile. Later on I want you to call Sonny, and he will come walk you to the diner. I'm going to have Sonny help me change all the locks on the house when our shifts over. I don't want you here alone until its done."

"Okay, but I will go to the hardware store and get all new locks so its ready when you get off work." I silence his lips. "I won't go alone. I will have Emily go with me, and we will be careful."

"Carrie."

"Don't worry, we'll be safe. I can't just stay behind closed doors. I need to get out, I need to get a job soon. I know you want to protect me, and I love you for it."

"Carrie.."

"Shh please, just hear me okay. I need to be useful. I want to help. I'll take my taser gun." I smile to try and lighten the moment.

After serious kissing, and promises to be safe I finally get Chance to leave Nana's. Emily meets me out front to go to the hardware store.

"Lets go get my truck because I want to go clothes shopping before the hardware store. I didn't mention it to Chance because I want to surprise him."

"What could you possibly want to buy here?" Emily squeals as we pull up to the women boutique store.

"I need new underwear." I stare at her.

"Sexy new underwear." She giggles.

"Its been a long time since I have wanted to please my man."

"Sweet."

"Are you getting anything?" She is browsing some risque racks.

"I'm going to lay a few things on the line for a certain someone, and maybe wearing something very sexy under my clothes will help my courage." She holds up a see through pair of black thongs, and bra set in one hand. Garters, and stockings in the other.

"Worst case scenario, you strip, leave, and let him see what he's missing while dealing with a hard on from hell!"

"I like the way you think." Her devious expression says it all as she heads for the checkout.

"Oh yeah."

We get plenty of new locks from the hardware store before heading to the diner. We hide our bags behind my seat in the truck before we enter the diner.

We order a late lunch.

"You never did tell me why the lock changes." Emily grabs my hand. "Is this about the poisoning?"

"Yes, and I received some photos in the mailbox today." I explain everything that has happened since I arrived.

"Here is your order by special delivery." Chance kisses me after putting our plates down.

"I got all the new locks. Emily is going to come over, and we are going to cook for you and Sonny while you change the locks."

"I'll grill while you make a salad." Emily quickly says.

"Hey! Does everybody know I suck at cooking?" I laugh as Chance is trying very hard not the laugh.

"Seriously though Carrie, what all are the cops saying about this?" Emily seems worried.

"They looked over the house while Carrie was in the hospital. No evidence was left, not even a fingerprint. For now, changing the locks ,and being careful is all we can do." Chance sits beside me with his arm around me.

"That's bullshit, some sick fuck is messing with your lives, and you have to jump through hoops to be safe." Emily scoots over as Sonny sits down.

"We have about ten minutes before we have to be back in the kitchen. Dinner prep needs started. How are you holding up Carrie?" Sonny leans over Emily, and squeezes my fingers.

"I'll feel better when you two have all the locks changed. That photo was about all I got left. Its my fucking body, and knowing someone was there, in my most private moment, makes me sick." I can still see it clearly.

"What photo?" Sonny asks.

"I told him you got photos in the mail, but I didn't mention that particular one. I didn't know if you wanted me too." Chance cups my cheek.

"Its fine, I trust them." I lean into his palm feeling my eyes water.

"Someone took a photo of her in the shower inside our house. This is your home now, and I won't allow some sick fuck to screw it up." His lips are soft, and sweet against mine. "Be safe baby." Chance gets up to go back to work.

"I'll see you ladies in a few hours." Sonny keeps his eyes on Emily, as he leaves the table.

Emily and I head back over to Nana, and Grandpas for awhile.

"You girls need to come out here, and let her rest now." Grandpa pulls us out from Nana's room after two hours of pampering her.

"Has it really been two hours?" I look at the clock on the wall.

"Nana is excited to get to meet Destiny, Nick, and Alexa this weekend. She is going to spoil Destiny rotten." Emily laughs because Grandpa is already preparing for it by digging out some of Emily's childhood toys.

"Its been along time since we've had a young one around here." Grandpa hugs me. "Nana will love it."

"I'm excited to see Justine again. That woman is a riot."

"Emily, you just want her to kick Crystals ass."

"Well, if she shows up, and continues to hit on your man then its her own fault." Emily laughs at her own reasoning.

"Lets go get the guys and get the grill fired up. We'll send some over for you two." We leave after hugging.

We are walking slowly towards the diner, enjoying the sunshine, and talking about this upcoming weekend when a truck pulls right up in front of us slamming on its breaks.

"What the fuck!" I jump back.

"Crystal. You bitch! What the hell do you want? You almost hit us." Emily screams, smacking the side of her truck.

"I just left the diner, and I must say the service was quite satisfying." Crystal laughs as her eyes meet mine while pulling away.

I just continue heading toward the diner. I'm not going to let that skank get to me even though I feel my guts churning inside.

"Ignore that bitch, she's just trying to get a rise out of you. Chance doesn't want her ass, and she is pissed about it." Emily squeezes my hand.

I smile to ease the tension, and head into the diner. I don't head to the kitchen with Emily. I need a few moments to myself, so I head toward the restroom.

I wash my face, and breathe in a few times to stop myself from crying before I head back out.

"Hi babe." Chance grabs my hand then kisses me.

"You ladies ready to head out?" Sonny grabs the bag of locks out of the back.

"Did we get exactly what we needed?" Emily nods toward the bag.

"Perfect."

I head out with Chance at my back. Emily grabs our bags out of the truck, and I follow Sonny inside after unlocking the front door.

"You're being very quiet tonight." Sonny bumps my shoulder looking concerned.

"I'm good, I'm just going to take a shower down here while you guys start the locks." I go grab some sweats, a tee shirt, and undergarments out of the dryer.

"You okay, you seem upset." Chance grabs me before I shut the door.

"Just stress. I'm okay, really." I kiss him. "Go help Sonny, and I'll be quick." I close the door.

Until all the locks are changed I'm more comfortable using this bathroom. I need to let that bullshit Crystal pulled go because if I don't she is getting what she wants. Chance didn't say anything about her, so I need to trust him that everything is fine.

I throw my wet hair up into a ponytail, and throw on my comfy clothes before I head into the kitchen where I see onto the patio that Emily has steaks on the grill.

I grab two tall glasses, and mix up some Jack and Coke. I need something to relax me.

I pull up a lounge chair on the patio, and start sucking down my drink.

"Is one of those for me?" Emily laughs at me gulping one down.

"Yes, if you agree to the next refill." I lean my head back.

"Whatever you need." She sits down beside me looking concerned.

"I'm fine Emily I just need to forget about everything for awhile."

We sit in silence for awhile, and I'm on my second big drink. I'm not feeling much of anything.

"The foods ready Carrie. I think maybe you should eat something." She laughs as I stumble trying to get up.

"Damn, I'm feeling pretty good."Laughing, I plop my ass down in a kitchen chair as soon as we get inside.

My partial bottle of Jack is still sitting on the table. I reach for it, but Chance grabs it first. He looks at how much is left then turns his eyes toward me with a smile. "Are you girls having a good time?" He hands it to Sonny.

"Hey! Give that back." I lunge for it, but Sonny holds it up too high for me to reach.

"Babe, you need to eat." Chance pulls my chair back for me.

"I will, just give me the bottle, and I promise to eat my steak." I jump up and snatch it from Sonny's hand while he isn't looking.

"Damn woman." Sonny laughs.

"I was a gymnast in school." I wink at Sonny before sitting down beside Chance.

"Eat up sweetheart."

"Okay." I eat as much as I can to please everyone while still finishing up my drink.

"Feeling better?" Emily asks me quietly while the guys are talking.

I shrug my shoulders because I don't know if I feel like laughing or crying. I lean toward Emily. "That fucker never did let me have very many friends. Well, at least not while he wasn't around to supervise." I mumble quietly.

"He was a fucking asshole Carrie. He didn't deserve you." Emily squeezes my hand.

"That no good asshole fucked so many women behind my back. I don't get it. I feel so .... This shit has to stop. Why can't people leave me alone, and stop trying to take my happiness. I don't like this feeling of feeling out of control." I feel dizzy, and fucking emotional.

"How strong was that last drink girl?" Emily leans toward me, but she's kind of blurry.

"I bought sexy underwear. Hey, did you get them out of the trunk.... truck?" I try to stand up.

"Come on babe, its time for bed." Chance is carrying me.

"I think I drank too much." I giggle. "Shit, I'm spinning." My head feels fuzzy. I hear laughter then warm blankets come around me. Then darkness.

I wake up feeling nauseous and my head is pounding. I go down to the kitchen for a drink, and some aspirin. The water feels so good on my throat. I need to pee so bad, so I head for the bathroom off the kitchen. I relive myself, and as I head back into the hallway I hear moaning coming from the spare bedroom.

What the hell. Its still dark outside and my brain isn't fully functioning yet. I quietly push open the door to the guestroom, and the light from the hall shows me a bare ass pounding away at someone. It hits me that it is Sonny, and Emily. Holy shit. I quickly shut the door, but not before an image of an eagle forms in my mind from Sonny's back, and the talons go down to wrap around his hips. That was hot as fuck.

I hurry upstairs, and crawl in to Chance's backside to snuggle up to.

I have no idea what time it is when I make my way downstairs, but its daylight.

I see the clock and groan. What the hell am I doing awake at seven thirty in the morning. I smell coffee as I make my way downstairs to the kitchen where Emily and Chance are sitting.

"Coffee." I mutter as I get a cup. I stay standing against the counter till I have a second refill in my cup. I sit down, but no one has said a word. They just stare at me. "What?" I look between the two of them. "What?" I ask again. I feel my grumpy ass getting irritated. I get up to fill my cup for the third time, and still nothing. "Whatever." I turn my back . I take a deep breath. "Somebody better start talking before I start yelling. This silence is fucked up." I turn back to them feeling my eyes water.

"I love you Carrie." Emily hugs me then heads into the hallway.

I look to Chance.

"You talk a lot in your sleep Carrie. Especially after all the alcohol last night." Chance is looking pissed.

"I can't control that. Are you mad at me or something?" I am genuinely confused.

"Mad at you? Jesus Christ Carrie" Chance stands up, and pulls me into a chair beside him. "You were crying in your sleep. You were begging someone to stop, and I don't think it was from the attack you told me about."

"I don't remember dreaming or anything. Why are you so upset?"

"Did Alex ever..... did he ever make you have sex when you didn't want to?"

I feel myself stiffen. I try to stand up but Chance puts his arms around my back to lean into me.

"We were married, he expected things so in the beginning it was okay, but when I started smelling the women on him, I just..... He had photos of them...." I turn my head.

"Carrie."

"I didn't want to but ..... This shit is in the past! Please..... I." He pulls me onto his lap.

"I know he is Alexa's father, but I want to rip his fucking head off." Chance holds me tight.

"Can we just forget this shit please."

"Can you tell me why you decided to drink so much last night?"

"All the shit that's been happening lately. I guess I just had enough." I lay my head on his shoulder.

"Emily told me about that shit with Crystal yesterday."

I stiffen up. "She is just trying to piss me off."

Chance grabs my chin and pulls my eyes to his. "There has been no one since you, and there will never be anyone but you. I need you to trust me."

"I know. I don't know why I let her bother me. My fucking insecurities get the best of me sometimes. I do trust you, please know that. It isn't about you when I feel this way. I have been through hell in my life and I'm a lot stronger than I use to be. I just have bad days. I am working on it."

"She can't come between us if we don't let her. I love you Carrie."

"I love you too."

"So, where are the sexy underwear you bought?"

"Hey, that was supposed to be a surprise!" I laugh when his eyebrows go up and down.

"You talk a lot." His hands go up under my shirt.

I moan from the pleasure of his hands on my breast.

"You ready Uncle Chance?" Emily steps into the kitchen with Sonny.

"Your timing sucks girl." Chance pulls his hands out from under my shirt.

"Yeah, people walking in on your action can suck." Emily winks at me and I'm sure my face is ten shades of red.

"I have to cook till noon, and Emily will be on till two, but Sonny is free. I hope you don't mind, but he is going to hang out here."

"I don't want to take you from your day off Sonny. The locks are changed, and I will be fine."

"Hey, you and me today. We'll have a blast, don't worry about it Carrie." Sonny turns and kisses Emily with heat.

"About damn time." Chance mutters before he kisses me. "I love you baby." Let Sonny help me by being here okay. I won't worry so much."

"Hurry back to me." I kiss him.

"What kind of trouble do you want to get into today?" Sonny rubs his hands together like an excited little kid.

We spend the first couple of hours talking about his Gamma's cooking, and playing cards.

"I'm going to shower then maybe we could take a walk. I need to get out for some fresh air."

"I'll use the downstairs shower then meet you back here." Sonny heads down the hall.

I grab a skirt, blouse, and one of my new underwear outfits. I'm just finishing combing the rats out of my wet hair when I hear Sonny hollering.

"What?" I step out in the hallway at the top of the stairs.

"I said are you about ready?" He is laughing at me.

"What's so funny?"

"Look down."

"Oh well hell." I laugh at myself as I realize my blouse is inside out.

I step back into the bedroom and fix my blouse before heading downstairs.

"That's better."

"Oh shut up." I laugh as I grab my sweater.

"Where to my lady?" Sonny holds out his arm.

"Anywhere."

We walk for awhile just enjoying the peace and quiet.

"I really am sorry that you have to spend your day off with me instead of doing whatever you had planned."

"No plans, just staying at home either working on my truck, or fixing my toaster. The piece of shit is burning my toast. "

"Okay." I smile. He makes me feel as if I'm not a bother. Most of my life, other than my daughter, people always made me feel as if I'm in the way. "Sonny?"

"Yeah."

"Thanks for being my friend." I squeeze his arm.

"No thanks needed Darlin', you're easy to love. I wasn't kidding when I said Chance was one lucky son of a bitch."

I feel my eyes watering. I have found love, and real friendship here in this town. Justine has been my only true friend until now. Now I have my love, and two more friends.

"Lets go to the park." Sonny guides me across the street to the swings.

"Are you serious?" I ask as he holds a swing still for me.

"Yes, I'm serious. Why not?" He starts pushing me. "You love Chance, and I haven't seen him laugh as much as I have since you finally called him. When you were gone, he was miserable. Hell, even I thought he was crazy to fall for someone so quick, but I've seen you two together. You make him happy, so I like you." Sonny continues to push me.

I feel very emotional with his words. I feel wonderful, and loved. "I like you too." I barely get the words out, feeling choked up. I needed this day. It feels normal and stress free.

"Do you want to go get coffee?" Sonny stops my swing.

"Sure, the diner?"

"Yep."

"You missing Emily?" I smile when his neck flushes red.

"Come on troublemaker." He laughs as he puts his arm around me to head back toward the diner.

We walk in and the place is full of regulars, and a few people I haven't seen before.

"Looks like we better get two coffees to go." I look around but there is no seats available.

"Come on." He pulls me toward the kitchen. "Go give lover boy a kiss, and I'll get the coffees." He heads toward Emily who is swamped.

I walk in the kitchen where Chance is very busy getting food prepared. He doesn't notice me, so I sneak up and stand off to the side to watch him. He is very skilled, cooking as if his mind is on auto pilot. Never slowing down, just piling plates, flipping eggs, and pancakes all at the same time.

I watch his muscles flex, and his butt twist as he works. When my eyes travel back up his body his eyes are staring at me with a smirk on his face. He knows I was checking him out.

"Hey baby."

"I don't want to get in your way, I just came to steal a kiss while Sonny grabs us coffee." I step up, and kiss him openly for a few seconds, then step back. "Now get back to work." I smack his ass.

"Yes Ma'am." He licks his lips.

I go back out of the kitchen to find Sonny, but I don't see him. I don't see Emily either. They probably slipped off somewhere to neck. I smile thinking about them, probably out back or in the restroom.

I step outside to call Justine while I wait for Sonny.

"Hey girl, what's up?"

"Are you still coming here to see me?"

"I'll be there tomorrow actually. Its a day early, but I didn't figure that you would mind. Surprise!" She laughs.

"Fuck yes, that's great! I miss my best friend."

"How are you?"

"I'm..." I hesitate.

"Don't bullshit me either. How are you?" Her no nonsense approach always makes me know this is my best friend, and I can tell her anything.

"I've had a few problems with that Crystal bitch from the clothing store, and a few things I'd rather talk to you in person about."

"I'm going to beat that whores ass. Just say the word."

"I miss you." I whisper. I need her, I need my best friend. "Hurry."

"I'll be there by noon tomorrow."

"I love you."

"Back at ya."

"There you are. Your coffee is getting cold." Sonny hands me a large cup. "Hey, are you okay?" He looks at my tear filled eyes.

"I will be." I grab his arm, and head toward home.

We head into the kitchen where I watch him prepare homemade chicken salad for sandwiches. Its interesting to watch him cook because he makes it seem so easy.

I enjoy more coffee in the peace and quiet of the kitchen. I'm so tired. As time goes by I feel my head lowering to the table, and I tell myself I will just rest for a minute.

"She's exhausted."

"So tell me what else is going on."

"Listen Sonny, I can't give you specifics, but her ex is a real asshole who treated her like she was nothing. Now, she's dealing with a psycho who wants to hurt her. Nobody here knows her, so it has to be someone from her other life in Ohio."

"What about Crystal? She wants you back man."

"She never had me. She was a fucking one night drunken stand. I've tried to be nice, and tell her I'm not interested, but she won't leave me alone. I haven't even looked at another woman since I met Carrie that first morning. Besides, she wouldn't be smart enough to do all that shit."

"Not by herself." Sonny says.

"Are you two done?" I interrupt because my head hurts, and I don't want to think about Crystal.

"Hey sleepyhead." Chance kisses me as he rubs my shoulders.

"I have a headache." I rub my temples.

"Let me help with that." Chance pulls me up, and into the living room.

He sits down sideways on the couch, and leans back onto the arm of the sofa. He pulls me down with my back against his chest, and massages my temples.

"Justine will be here tomorrow, and Alexa will be here Saturday with Destiny, and Nick." I relax into him.

"Have you told Justine anything yet?"

"Some, but if I tell her the worst on the phone she would have already been here, Nobody better warn Crystal that she is coming. I want to see the look on her face when she sees her." I smile.

"I knew you had some evil in you. Hell yeah, after Emily told me about Justine in the clothing store even I want to see Crystals face." Sonny laughs from the doorway.

"What happened in the clothing store?" Chance looks between Sonny and I.

"Lets just say Justine doesn't take kindly to people being cruel to me, and she has a temper from hell." I smile.

"Cruel how?" Chance pulls my chin around.

"About my size." I shrug.

"Shit, shes just jealous your fucking hot, and she looks like a crack whore with big tits." Sonny laughs. "Hey!" He hollers when a pillow hits him in the face.

I laugh, feeling relaxed listening to them two bicker.

"Music to my ears baby." Chance kisses me on the back of my head.

"Do you like the new coffee pot Carrie?"

"I really appreciate you and Emily getting us a new one."

"Nobody wants to see you without your coffee." Sonny smiles at me while blocking another pillow that I throw at his face.

"Smart ass." I stand up from the couch. "I need to finish up a few chapters while some ideas are fresh in my mind. Thanks for the massage." I kiss Chance.

"Chapters?" Sonny looks confused.

"She's a writer. I thought I told you."

"Hell no, you didn't. I would have remembered something like that. What do you write about Carrie?"

"She writes smut." Chance's eyes are excited.

"Gymnast, and a writer of filth. You lucky fucker!" Sonny laughs. "I want to read some of your work."

"No!"

"No!" Chance, and I yell at the same time. "And as far as being a gymnast, that was a hell of a long time ago." I shake my head at him. "I'll see you around Sonny, and thanks for today." I kiss his cheek, and head upstairs to write.

Chance

Its late, and Carrie went to bed a few hours ago, but I just can't sleep. With all the crazy shit that has been happening to Carrie lately, I feel on edge.

Someone was in my fucking house. Thinking about it makes me angry. I know we changed all the locks, and done everything we can to make things safe, but I'm worried because I can't be with her twenty four seven. Some psycho is after her, and my gut tells me its her sick fucking ex.

"Chance?" Carrie is standing at the top of the stairs in my shirt looking sinfully sexy, and half asleep.

"Yeah babe?"

"Come to bed."

"I'll be right up honey." I triple check all the doors, and windows before I head upstairs.

I crawl into bed, and curl my body around her. I hear her sigh, as I drift off to sleep.

I wake to an empty bed. I stretch out my limbs before I grab my sleeping pants, and shirt off the floor. I head down stairs. Today is my day off, and I don't want to waste it sleeping all day.

I find Carrie, and Justine sitting at the kitchen table drinking coffee.

"Hey baby." I kiss Carrie good morning. "How are you Justine?" I grab myself some coffee before I sit down, and that's when I notice Justine's eyes are red and puffy from crying.

"I'm glad I'm here." She squeezes Carrie's hand.

"Alex has been hounding her everyday for information about me. Rather I'm happy, or miserable in my new home." Carrie looks disgusted.

"You've seen him in person a lot lately?" I need to be sure.

"Yes, the asshole even showed up at my home. I thought for sure Greg was going to kill him before I could get him to leave." Justine grabs Carrie's hand. "I did get one last parting shot in to his ego when he pulled away. I told him Carrie was very happy with her boy toys big ten inch cock." She laughs so hard she snorts.

The women high five, and I can't help but smirk as I shake my head.

"If its not Alex pulling this shit then who the fuck is trying to hurt you?" I run my hand down my face in frustration.

"Why the hell am I getting photos of you with other women in the past, and why a photo of me taking a shower? It makes no sense."

"Is it someone who is jealous of your relationship with Chance because my money is on that bitch Crystal."

"I agree." Carrie says, looking at me.

"What do you want to do? Any ideas?" I ask.

"I'll beat the answers out of her, just give me ten minutes alone with her."

"Pull your claws back in Justine. I don't want you in jail." Carrie smiles at her friend.

"Everyone will be at the diner Saturday, right?" Justine asks Carrie.

"Yes, all friends, and family are welcome. Sonny, Chance's friend, who is also Em's man ,is cooking for us. You'll meet him sometime today, he is so sweet. He promised to serve up some special recipes that his Gamma use to make."

"Would you stop saying the man is sweet, or at least don't let him hear it, or I'll never hear the end of it." I growl at her because I know she is going to say it to him, just because she loves to see us bicker.

"Is he as hot as Chance is?" Justine winks at Carrie.

"Oh yeah."

"Hey!" I pull Carrie off her chair into my lap. "I'm going to spank that ass." I nip her earlobe.

"Promises, Promises." Carrie slowly wiggles her ass around until I'm fucking hard.

"So Justine, did your husband not come along?" I try to ignore Carries sweet ass rubbing me.

"He's over at the hotel, he'll be here shortly. I let him sleep in a little since I made him leave while it was still dark out to get here as soon as we could. Once he finds out all you've told me I'll be lucky to take a piss by myself while we're here."

"Well, I for one can understand that feeling." I squeeze Carrie to me.

"You said everyone will be at the diner tomorrow, so lets set a trap here while we are over there." Justine looks to me.

"What kind of trap? I mean, I'm willing to try anything as long as it doesn't involve Carrie being put in harms way."

"Well duh, but I was thinking maybe I can get Greg to hide out in your house to keep an eye on Carrie's unlocked truck. Its worth a shot, and trust me that Greg can take care of himself. He knows how much Carrie means to me. That alone puts Carrie in his protection."

The doorbell rings.

"That's probably him now." Justine goes to let him in, and I'm right behind her with Carrie in tow.

The first thing he does is kiss her hard. I look over at Carrie and she is smiling really big at them.

"Greg, how are you?" Carrie walks around me with her arms open.

I growl under my breath when he picks her up, and hugs her.

"Its really good to see you Carrie, and its really good to be here without the kids." Greg puts her down. "I'm Greg, and you must be Chance. Its nice to finally put a face with the name." He shakes my hand hard. "Has he been treating you good Carrie?" He asks her, but is still looking at me.

"I've never felt more loved." Carrie steps back under my arm.

I look down at her looking up at me, and I can't help myself. I kiss her.

"That's what I figured because other wise you would have already been in Justine's sights." Greg laughs as he pulls Justine back to him.

"Come on in and sit down so we can fill you in on what Carrie has already discussed with Justine." I pull Carrie down onto the couch with me.

We go over everything that's happened with Greg, and he is simmering with anger. He appears calm but the tick in his jaw tells me he is not.

"You don't need to ask me if I'll stay here, its already guaranteed, but I do have one problem."Greg looks to Justine.

"Honey, I will be in the diner with Carrie, and everyone else. I won't go anywhere on my own."

"I mean it Justine, I will take your ass home right now." He covers her mouth when she begins to protest. "I know you woman, and yes, I know you can handle yourself, but just this once please promise me."

Justine reaches up, and kisses the worry on his face. "I promise." She covers his mouth with her fingers. "But" She smiles when he rolls his eyes. "You call me as soon as anything happens. No hero shit, just get pictures."

"I'll call Chance first, then you." He looks over at me with respect.

"Greg...."

"Babe, if it were you, I need to know first. I'm sure Chance would appreciate it."

"You and Carrie will be the first people I turn to if he calls with anything. I would do this myself if I could , but whoever is doing this will be sure we are all over at the diner, and assume my house is empty."

"I know, I just have a bad feeling." Justine leans back onto Greg's lap.

We spend most of the day in the garage playing pool, bullshitting, and checking over Carrie's truck. Greg helps me change the oil, and give it a tune up.

"We're heading inside you boys enjoy yourselves tinkering around under that hood." Carrie and Justine leave us to ourselves.

"So, Justine said Alex has been hounding her about Carrie." Now that we're alone I want to hear his thoughts on Alex.

"Yeah, that piece of shit knows she is in a relationship with you now. He never really bothered her because she never dated anyone since the divorce. Now, he thinks he has the right. He really believes she will come back to him, or at the very least get tired of you."

"She'll never go back to that kind of hell, she's a much stronger woman now. Fucker better be careful before he crosses the wrong person." I just stare at him because I know he understands my meaning.

"I know Justine says she has seen him around a lot lately, but its eight hours from there, and that's doable. We'll find out something tomorrow."

"I really appreciate your help on this." I know I don't have to say anything because its for Carrie, but I want him to know I give a shit.

"If it hurts that woman in there, I'll do anything to fix it because if I don't that would hurt my Justine. That's not an option."

"You ever need anything you let me know."

"You got it. I do have one more thing to ask." He leans up to get my attention.

"Justine trusts me when she confides in me. I would never betray that trust." He gets up and paces the floor.

I wait till he is ready to ask whatever is on his mind.

"I also know a person should be well informed."

"Give me a hypothetical situation." I try to give him a way to inform me without betraying Justine.

"Suppose someone you love has nightmares and they talk in their sleep." He looks at me.

"I know."

He nods in understanding.

"Do you have any kids Chance?"

"No, and I'm okay with that. She's worried that I will change my mind about it."

"Will you?"

"No" I don't need to say anything else.

"Did you meet her daughter yet?"

"We stopped in Tennessee for a few hours."

"That right there should tell you she's all in."

I smile like a fool in love. "That granddaughter of hers sure is a sweetheart. We're going to go to her riding competition in a few weeks."

"She'll have you wrapped around her little finger."

"Two hours in her company, and she already does." I laugh feeling much lighter.

Greg seem like a really nice guy. Kind, protective, and all about his family. A man I can respect.

"You guys come on in for some dinner." Justine hollers.

"I hope Carrie didn't cook." Greg whispers.

I laugh clapping him on the back in understanding.

We enjoy a meal of steak, baked potatoes, corn on the cob, and ice cream for dessert.

We're all sitting around enjoying a movie when there is loud banging on the front door.

"What the hell." I open the door to a drunk Sonny. "Easy man." I grab him before he falls down.

"Sonny?" Carrie helps get him to the kitchen table before starting coffee.

"Where's Em?" I try to get him to focus on me.

"Drink some coffee Sonny." Carrie sits beside him with a big cup of coffee.

"Thanks Carrie at least you don't hate me." He slurs but I can still understand him.

"Did you and Emily have a fight or something?" The mother in Carrie is soothing his hair in comfort.

"I told her that I love her, and she slammed the door in my face." I barely hear the words he chokes out.

"Drink your coffee then we'll talk some more." Carrie shoves the coffee in him.

After two full cups, and mumbling about words Emily supposedly said he speech is finally a little better.

"Why is she angry with you Sonny? Emily loves you, and I know damn well she'd be happy for you to tell her you love her. So, what the hell did you do?" I demand because Emily is my niece and I can't stand the thought of her hurting.

"Crystal stopped me, and begged me to tell you that she needs to talk to you. I told her to leave you alone. I started to turn around to walk away, but she grabbed my arm. When I turn back toward her she got up in my space real close. She whispered in my ear that she would be seeing you real soon. I just said whatever, and I turned to leave but Emily was standing outside. She looked madder than hell. She won't let me explain. I caught up with her at her door and you know the rest."

I smack him in the back of the head.

"What the fuck Chance!" Sonny hollers and stumbles trying to stand up.

"So, instead of just staying outside of her door, never giving up, you go get drunk. Real smart dumb ass." I shake my head in disgust at his explanation.

"Don't do that again Chance!" Sonny pushes my chest all pissed off.

"Oh hell no!" Carrie gets right in between us. She shoves her finger into my chest. "Try to be a little more understanding." She turns toward Sonny. "You need to get your shit together, sober up, and shower. If either one of you ever let that bitch Crystal come between you or anyone you love again I will slap the shit out of you both. Now, Justine and I are going over to Emily's." Carrie stomps off muttering about bullheaded stupid men.

"You best get to it Sonny before she comes back." Justine, and Greg are smiling as they stand in the kitchen doorway. "I'm Justine by the way, and this is my husband Greg."

"Hi" Sonny mumbles as he heads for the shower.

We all stand around laughing until Carrie walks back in then we all quiet down.

"We good?" I pull her into my arms.

"Yes, but I want to go see Emily. Come on Justine." She kisses me.

"We'll walk you two over." I insist.

"Okay, but then come back here, and talk to Sonny, he's hurting."

"Okay" I kiss her. "I love you."

"I love you too."

We drop the ladies off with orders to lock the door, and keep their cell phones ready.

When Greg and I enter my kitchen after returning Sonny is just coming from the shower looking more sober.

"Feeling better?"

"Yeah" Sonny sits down looking pretty depressed.

"Good now let me remind you, as long as Carrie is having problems with some psycho you stay sober to help protect her, or I will beat the fucking shit out of you. We clear?" I stare at him hard.

"Yes Sir." Sonny looks back at me with shame.

"Now that we're on the same page let me say this, Emily loves you. She will come around and let you explain, but she's hurting right now. You do have a reputation for being a playboy."

"I haven't....." He starts to interrupt.

"I know you haven't okay, but people talk about all the women in your past, and Emily hears that shit at work. You need to tell her the complete truth."

"I will, but I haven't been with anyone in over a year. Emily and I are still new at this relationship, and I don't want to fuck it up."

"I know you are a good man Sonny, and I know you would never cheat on her."

"Never"

"I'd cut your balls off, literally."

"I'd give you the knife." Sonny's eyes are all red but he is listening.

"I need to go see her, make her understand that I would never hurt her."

"Let the women talk with her for awhile first. Trust a man who has been married a long time." Greg joins in on the conversation.

"Nice to meet you Greg." Sonny finally shakes his hand.

"You too Sonny." Greg refills Sonny's coffee.

We sit around talking about tomorrow evenings dinner at the diner, some of the things Sonny will be cooking, and the plans of Greg hopefully catching on film whoever the hell is messing with Carrie.

I'm making a fresh pot of coffee when I hear the front door being opened. I step into the front room just as the women enter.

"Why the fuck didn't you call, you shouldn't be walking out there in the dark!" Greg is in Justine's space in seconds, and he is one pissed off big man.

"Listen caveman......." Justine squeals as Greg throws her over his shoulder, and slaps her on the ass hard.

"Damn right I'm a caveman......." Greg's words cut off as he slams the door behind them.

"Holy shit!" Sonny says.

"Don't worry she can handle it." Carrie is laughing till she turns, and sees that I am staring at her, but I'm not laughing. "Are you pissed too?" She wraps her arms around my neck.

"Yes." I bend down and squeeze her ass cheeks in my hands before lifting her up, and having her legs wrap around my waist. "Work that shit out Sonny." I holler at Sonny on my way upstairs with my woman.

I head straight to the shower and close the door behind us.

"We have guest downstairs." Carrie mutters.

I ignore that and start stripping her clothes off.

"Chance?"

When we're both naked, and the water is set I pull her under the water with me. I get down on both knees in front of her. I bury my face into her belly. I'm tired of all the things that are happening, of all the fear I have inside of losing her, of someone taking her from me.

I begin to slowly kiss her body all the way up and down her wet skin, but purposely skip all the areas her body is begging me to kiss.

She doesn't believe that little walk they did was a problem. Its foolish for her to put herself at risk even for a second.

"Chance?"

I feel myself trembling as she runs her hands through my hair. I'm trying to get my fear under control. I bury my face in her side. I've seen some of the cruel things people can do in this world. I can't lose my soul.

"You have to be more careful."

"I wasn't trying to worry you. It was a quick two minute walk, and I wasn't alone."

I kiss my way up her belly in between her breasts then pull her nipple into my mouth, and suck hard.

"Fuck" She leans her head back onto the shower wall.

I slowly run my fingers up her inner thigh and over the top of her pussy. I barely skim my fingers through her slit, as I continue to alternate between her breasts.

"Chance please." She moans, pushing her pussy harder against my fingers, trying to get me inside of her.

I lift her leg around my hip so I can push my cock against her, but not in her yet. "You have to be more careful." I rub the head through her slit and pinch her nipple at the same time.

"Please."

"I can't lose you Carrie." I take her mouth as I finally push up inside of her hard and fast.

I lose control, and pound up into her over, and over. My head feels like it wants to explode when my body empties inside of her.

She just holds me, as I catch my breath, and pull myself together.

I pull myself free of her and grab the soap to wash her.

I quickly wash myself then turn off the shower. I grab towels and dry us off. After wrapping us in towels I pull her by the hand to our bed.

"Chance."

"Shhh." I grab a brush and pull her between my legs. I slowly start to work out the rats trying not to hurt her head. "My mom died giving birth to me witch left me with my piece of shit father. He left me with his parents when I was six years old. He abandoned me and never looked back. My mom told my Nana that the only reason she didn't abort my ass was because she planned on selling me. My father said I wasn't worth the hassle. Nana, and Grandpa became my parents." I braid her hair then turn to ease her back onto the bed. "I don't remember a lot about him other than I went hungry a lot, and I slept in a cold car many times while he gambled our money away."

"I'm grateful for your Nana and Grandpa. The best thing he did was give you up." Carrie soothes me.

"I only have a small circle of people in my life that I love. Losing one of them will hurt like hell, but you Carrie, losing you will kill me. You have to be more careful." I squeeze my eyes shut, and lay my head on her chest.

"I'm sorry, I promise I'll be more careful." Her hands run through my wet hair.

I start kissing her fingers as I pull them to my mouth. I suck one into my mouth. I release her finger then sit up, and reach over to the side table to pull out four scarves. Her eyes go hot as I tie her to the bed.

"Are you enjoying yourself?"

"I love your laugh baby." I open her towel up to stare down at her body. I run my hands up her inner thighs. "I'm going to feast on you until you beg me to stop. I'm so hungry for your taste in my mouth." I start kissing up her legs.

"You already started in the shower. Can't you skip ahead?" She begs by pushing up her hips to get me where she wants me.

"Not yet." I rise up above her. "Give me those lips."

"Chance!" Sonny is pounding on our bedroom door.

"Are you fucking kidding me?" I growl out in frustration.

"Sorry man, its important."

"Fuck" I quickly release the scarves and drop my towel. I slide on my sleep pants and a tee shirt.

As soon as Carrie is clothed I open my door.

"What could be so important?" Sonny is standing with a paper bag.

"I went outside to, ah well, I went outside and this was at your door. It would have waited till morning, but ......" Sonny turns the bag around and there is a pregnancy test taped to the outside of the bag and it has a plus sign on it.

"You better have a good reason......" Carrie takes the bag from Sonny. Her face is stunned.

She reaches inside of the bag and pulls out a card. "Congratulations Daddy." She chokes. She reaches back into the bag and pulls out a photo of me in bed with a woman at the hotel. I'm drunk and passed out while the woman is hiding her face from the camera.

Carrie hands me the items and the bag then turns her back to me.

"Babe, this has to be a sick joke. Before I met you I've always used protection." I throw down the items, and grab her to me.

"Who's the woman?" She turns her head to look at me. "I bet I can guess."

"That's been over three months ago. It was once, and yes I was drunk, but I know I used protection. I'm very damn careful."

"Was there anything else in the bag?" Sonny leans down to pick it up. "Nothing."

"I need coffee I'm going down stairs."

"Babe, its late."

"I'm not sleeping anytime soon." Carrie takes off downstairs.

"Fuck" I grit my teeth and follow her.

"You okay?" Sonny quietly asks.

"As long as she doesn't leave me I'll get through anything." My fear of her leaving or being taken from me is still very real.

"Emily is asleep in the guest room."

"Are you two okay?" I ask him.

"We will be. That bitch Crystal seems to be causing trouble for both of us."

"You were going out to smoke weren't you?"

"I was thinking about it when I found that shit." He nods to the bag in his hand.

We walk in the kitchen where Carrie is in the middle of making coffee.

She has her back to me struggling with it when she drops the coffee. It goes

everywhere, and she leans down to clean it up.

"Let me help."

"I got it."

"Carrie."

"I said I got it!" She flings the container into the sink.

Her back is to me, but her hands are gripping the sink, and I can see her body silently

sobbing.

I don't say anything I just wrap my arms around her.

After a few moments she turns around and puts her arms around my neck.

"Don't leave me over this Carrie." I pick her up and sit her on the sink, and bury my face into her neck.

"Do you love me?"

"You know I do." I look up at her.

"Do you believe me when I tell you that I love you?"

"Yes."

"Then hold onto that while we figure this out." She wipes her eyes on my shoulder.

"Don't let that bitch come between you, or I'll have to knock some sense into you." Sonny repeats some of the words Carrie said to us before.

"That's pretty smart advice." Carrie smiles at Sonny.

"I'm a pretty smart guy."

"Smart ass!" I throw a dish towel at him.

"Go to bed you two, and I will clean this up. You're granddaughter doesn't need to see her Mamaw all tired out." Sonny begins cleaning up beside us.

"Thanks Sonny." Carrie leans over and kisses his cheek.

He wipes her cheek. "You're welcome doll face." He winks at her.

"Stop flirting with my girl." I pick her up and we head to bed with Sonny laughing behind us.

Carrie

We get upstairs and crawl into bed. No words are spoken between us. Chance is holding on to me tightly from behind. I know he's worried that I will leave him over this. I love him too much to ever do that, but if this pregnancy is real then my life has just gotten very complicated. If this is his child then I know he will make a damn good daddy. My fear is having to deal with Crystal. I know she wants him to be with her, but will she let him just be a dad to the baby without all the chaos from her. I doubt it.

"Babe, turn off your mind, and get some sleep." I feel his soft lips on the back of my neck.

I quietly lay here with a few tears escaping. I know he loves me, but I can't help the sorrow I feel at another woman giving him something that I can't. Its ripping at my insides. I remember the pure joy and love I felt when I looked at my baby girls eyes for the first time. Its a love like nothing else in the world. I want him to experience that, but can I really handle him experiencing that moment with out my emotions feeling betrayed. My mind isn't rational right now.

I spent most of the night half a sleep, and half awake. I feel like shit and the son is barely peeking in. The clock says its five fifty six a.m.

I ease out of bed trying not to wake Chance. I know he is tired. He laid there awhile before he finally crashed too.

I enter the kitchen and Emily is sitting there drinking coffee. I grab a cup and sit down beside her. That's when I notice she has that bag from last night. I look at her and she has been crying.

"Emily?" I take the bag and toss it down on the table.

"Please tell me you're not leaving Carrie. Chance would be devastated, and I would be too." She grabs my hand.

"I'm not, I just.....I ..." The fucking tears start again. "Oh god Emily, how the hell am I going to get through this? I can't give him that." I smack the bag across the table onto the floor.

She knows words won't help, so she pulls me into her arms, and just lets me cry it out. Then we continue drinking our coffee together in the quiet.

"I'm going to go take a shower then I need you to help me do my hair. Okay?" Emily squeezes my hand.

"I should go shower soon too." I laugh because my hairs a rats nest, and I'm still in my tee shirt and shorts.

"I'll help you with your hair too." Emily leaves me alone with my thoughts.

I get another cup of coffee, and go out in the back yard to sit at the patio. Its a little chilly but the fresh air smells so good. Its peaceful and quiet. This is what I want, no this is what I need in my life. I want to be at peace.

I don't know how long I sit here until someone tries to take my coffee cup.

"You're falling asleep." Sonny sits down beside me on my lounger. "What are you doing out here?"

"Its peaceful out here." I smile at him.

"You shouldn't be out here alone Carrie."

"I...." I shake my head not knowing how to explain.

He nudges for me to move over, and he leans back beside me. "When I first got home from overseas, I could only be comfortable in the silence. Loud noises would cause me to....... Well, I needed peace and quiet. My mind didn't want to settle, but I also figured out that when I was alone that my mind would go back there. It was hard to adjust to until I realized that talking about it helped me to learn to handle it better.. It takes time."

"I'm sorry you had to go through hell, but I'm also grateful for brave people like you, and Chance for keeping us safe. You're a good man Sonny." I squeeze his hand in mine.

"I'm also a very good listener if you ever need to bend my ear for awhile."

"Thank you for being my friend. I've never had very many people in my life who I could trust."

"Trust is hard to give."

"Yes, it is."

We sit for awhile in silence before Sonny speaks again.

"I can't ever give Emily a child." He turns his eyes to me, and the pain I see is overwhelming.

"Oh Sonny." I lean my head onto his shoulder.

"I was injured before I got sent stateside. I'm scarred down there. That's why I couldn't give into Emily loving me. It took her threatening to leave state for good before I finally broke down and told her my secret. She made me understand that her loving me wasn't about me giving her children. It was about her giving me total trust with her heart, and to keep it safe. I would love to give her a child, but I love her too much to ever give her up. I gave total trust of my heart to her to keep safe." He puts his arm around me for comfort. "You are the third person who knows this about me. I had to lay all my fears down for Emily last night, and that is true trust in someone. You need to tell Chance how scared you are, and let him have all your fears. Its the only way to truly trust someone with your heart."

"How did you get so wise?" I try to laugh, but it comes out as a sob.

"I had to be stupid first." He squeezes me. "I almost lost everything before I wised up. Don't let that happen to you Carrie. Chance is a damn good man."

"Thank you." I wipe my eyes, kiss his cheek, then head inside to get a long hot shower.

The house is so quiet as I grab some clothes for the day. I enter the bathroom and notice my eyes in the mirror.

"Damn" I turn and adjust the shower water.

I get in and just stand under the hot water, and let the tension ease out of my shoulders. I stay in as long as I can then get out and dry off.

First my sexy see through teal underwear, and bra set with lacy stockings, and garter belt to match. My black skirt that comes just above my knees, and my teal blouse. I apply a light dusting of makeup to cover the bags under my eyes.

I step into the bedroom to have Chance brush out my hair, but the bed is empty. Feeling a little disappointed I sit down on the edge of the bed, and brush it myself. I put a long braid in it. I slip on my boots and head downstairs.

"Chance?" I look around but no one is here. I check out back and still no one.

I go to the guest bedroom and knock. "Emily?" No one answers. I go to the kitchen and grab my cell phone off the counter. The battery is dead so I plug it in and put it on the counter.

While it is charging I hear muted voices coming from the garage door off the kitchen. I open the door, and as I go to step out I see Sonny and Emily on the tailgate of my truck. I smile as I quietly step back in the kitchen.

"What are you smiling about?" Chance nuzzles into my neck as he traps my body against the door.

I can feel how hard he is against my lower back. I push my ass back, and he leans down with his hips, and pushes himself up, and against my ass.

"I seem to keep catching them two in the middle of hot sex." I try to laugh, but it comes out as a moan.

"Hot sex huh, does watching them turn you on?" He cups my breast through my blouse and pinches my nipples.

"Yes" I lean my forehead onto the door. "You were gone when I got out of the shower." I reach around and pull his ass harder against me.

"I hit the shower down here so I could get ready for work. We're closing down early today for the dinner so I told Henry I would be there early this morning."

"You should have joined me." I turn around and take his mouth in a hot tongue scorching kiss.

"Fuck baby, I have to go." His forehead touches mine.

I pull back and really look at him. "Are you okay?"

He turns his head after kissing my forehead. "Yeah, just stressed I guess." He grabs a cup of coffee. "All this shit that's happening is getting on my nerves."

"I love you Chance." I feel like he is pulling away from me.

"I love you too."

"Then take five more fucking minutes and talk to me!" I'm feeling pissed at him stepping back.

"Carrie."

"No!" I grab his cup and sit it down. I push his ass into a kitchen chair.

My skirt is in the way so I pull it up enough to allow me to straddle his lap. "Now talk to me dammit. That's all I want!" I hold his chin.

He breathes in deeply. "I want you to feel you can talk to me first. I'm a selfish bastard when it comes to you." He seems pissed at me.

"I'm sorry I was quiet last night I just needed to think about my emotions first. I needed to work that shit through my mind." I put my forehead to his.

"I saw Sonny this morning while you were in the shower. I was going to join you after I used the toilet downstairs, but I ran into Sonny."

"Okay and......?" I'm confused at his emotions, then it hits me. "Chance" I pull his face up to mine.

"He said you were feeling emotional about this shit with Crystal. I was jealous that you didn't come to me with it I guess. I know its stupid, hell he's my brother in every way. I know you two are friends.... I mean I get that... Its just ...." He takes a breath and squeezes his eyes closed.

I pull his mouth to mine and kiss him hard. I pour all my love and emotions into this kiss for him. His hands hold my back tight to his front.

My cell phone starts chiming over and over with messages. I pull my mouth off his and look up at my phone.

"You need to get to the diner, but when you get back here we are going to have a long talk about everything. I love you with every breath in my body. My heart is totally in your trust." I put his hand over my heart.

He leans down and kisses me where his hand is. He parts my blouse to see my bra. "I love you too Carrie." A kiss between my breasts. "I'll cherish your heart." A kiss onto my left breast. "Above everything." A kiss onto my right breast. "And Everyone." His tongue slides from side to side. "Have this on and nothing else at noon when I get home in our bed all spread out for me." A bite of his teeth onto my nipple through my bra. "I want to worship you with my tongue and body before our talk." He takes my mouth while he pulls my blouse back into place.

When he finally pulls back I can't find my voice. I'm so fucking wet for him. I ache inside. I can feel my heartbeat clear down to my pussy.

He stands up with his arms around me and walks me to the counter. My skirt is still bunched up to right below my panties.

"You can't leave me like this Chance. I need....."

"I know what you need. You need to hold on tight." He quickly pulls my panties aside and shoves two fingers up inside of me hard.

"Oh god." I yell as my nails dig into his forearms.

"You are mine in every way Carrie." He bites my ear as his thumb flicks my clit.

I push my hips forward as my head slams backwards. I cry out when my juices flow out all over his fingers.

"You" He slams his fingers in. "Are" Slams his fingers again "Mine" And again one more time, curling his fingers. Hitting a spot that causes me to scream.

His mouth covers mine as I pour my orgasm out of me.

I literally fall forward onto his shoulder with my out of control breathing.

"I love you." He pulls back, pulls his fingers out, and into his mouth then sucks them clean. He puts my underwear back, pulls my skirt down, and then tenderly kisses me as my eyes tear up. "You are my world Carrie no matter what happens." He fixes my blouse as he stands me onto my wobbly legs. "See you in awhile." He kisses me again and heads to the diner.

I'm still standing in the same spot with my hair coming out of my braid, and my skirt all wrinkled up when Sonny and Emily come in from the garage.

"Well, well, well look who looks thoroughly ravished." Emily smirks at Sonny.

"Babe, you need to find a mirror." Sonny smacks her ass.

"Excuse me for a moment." I can feel my face getting hot, and laughter behind me when I run upstairs. My inner thighs are soaked with my cum. I need another shower.

I feel lighter and calmer as I shower off, and chose another set of clean clothes. A white set of underwear, another black skirt, and a white blouse will be just as sexy for Chance when he gets home.

I get downstairs and Emily has a brush, and some ribbons laying on the table. "Let me do your hair." She pulls out a chair for me.

"I'll do yours next."

"Awesome." She laughs when Sonny comes in and looks confused at all the hair accessories on the table. "Don't ask honey just sit down and enjoy the madness." Emily winks at him.

My cell phone begins chiming text after text again.

"Can you hand me that Sonny?" I take the cell from him.

My eyes must give away the shock I'm feeling when it says I have thirty three unopened messages.

"You okay?" Sonny sits down across from us.

I open the messages. Three are from Alexa letting me know when they left, half way here, and due to arrive in an hour, but the rest are from Alex.

"My daughter and her family will be here in about an hour. They left early." I start reading the ones from Alex next.

At first its how much he misses me, how much he's changed, and how much he wants me back. Then they become more angry, How dare I still be with the boy toy, he won't satisfy me long, then they all turn to how I'm a whore. I won't be able to keep a younger man for long, I'm too old to be starting over, and my daughter will never except another man to take her dads place.

I'm so disgusted by all his messages that I don't even realize Emily is all done with my hair, and Justine is here until she pulls my cell out of my hands.

"Block his ass Carrie." She hugs me.

"I know I need to, but I only keep his number in case of emergency or something with Alexa. He's still her father." I just shrug.

"You should tell Alexa about all the garbage he spews at you. Let her put him in his place." Justine sits beside me.

"She knows some of the stuff about how he treated me. Hell, she grew up around it, but I have shielded her from a lot of it. I'm not doing that to her."

"Carrie, I have an idea. Do you trust me to make this better for you?" Sonny asks.

"Sonny, I appreciate your help, but....."

"Do you trust me Carrie?" He won't let me answer anything else. "Your my friend, and Chance is like a brother. I loved, and trusted you both to help me when I was in need." He squeezes Emily's hand, "Now let me do the same for you."

"Yes, I totally trust you." I hand him my phone.

He begins tapping away and after a few minutes he gives it back. I open the messages and Alex's number has been blocked and deleted. I also see where he messages Chance. He forwarded Alex's phone number to Chance after telling Alex if he needs to get a hold of me about Alexa or our granddaughter then he has to do it through Chance's number.

"Thanks Sonny." I laugh, actually feeling more relieved.

"You're welcome doll face." He winks.

"Stop flirting with Chance's girl." Emily hits Sonny with a dish towel.

"Hey!" Sonny laughs as he chases Emily around the table.

"That's what Uncle Chance would have done!" She squeals as Sonny captures her.

We're all laughing and talking while I do Emily's hair, and then Justine tries to show me how to make a peach pie. The experience was fun, but when I tasted it I definitely wasn't impressed.

"Carrie, I was here the whole time how the hell did it turn out wrong?" Justine is laughing at me when I spit it into the trash can.

I walk over and look at all my ingredients. I start laughing, as I realize I used salt instead of sugar.

"Only you girl." Justine dumps the whole pie into the trash.

"Oh shut up." I rinse my mouth out at the bathroom sink.

Laughing, I head upstairs to use toothpaste to get the salt taste out of my mouth. My mouth is full of mouthwash when my phone chimes a message.

Unknown number. "Are you enjoying fucking his best friend?" I read the message aloud confused.

My messages are filling up with photos of Sonny pushing me on the swings, walking with his arm around me, us sitting close together with my head on his chest on the back patio.

"What the fuck?" Chance grabs my phone to see the photos better.

"Don't scare me like that!" I scream, grabbing my chest. "Fuck Chance, you almost gave me a heart attack."

He turns around without saying a word, and leaves the bedroom.

"Chance? Hey, where are you going?" I follow him down into the kitchen trying to keep up.

"She's mine!" He punches Sonny in the face, and knocks him to the floor. "Keep your fucking hands off her!" He is towering over Sonny.

I'm so shocked by his anger that I'm stunned into silence. My eyes water at the scene in front of me.

"What the fuck is wrong with you man?" Sonny gets up and wipes his mouth.

I'm jolted out of my silence by the betrayal on Sonny's face.

"Chance?" I grab his arm to spin him around. I'm so confused.

"Did you?" He asks with a quiet growl.

I feel like I've been slapped. A slap would have been better then the hurt that rushes through me. "You bastard!" I scream at his words. "You...." I turn and look at Sonny.

"I'm sorry that your kindness to me got between your friendship with your brother." I step up to Sonny and hug him before I turn toward the door.

"Carrie wait." Chance reaches out towards me.

I turn my head to look at him. "I gave you my complete trust, and my heart. I have nothing left to give." I grab my keys and head for the garage.

I open the door, hop in my truck, and leave. I can see everyone in the driveway yelling for me, but I've had enough. I need to be alone for awhile. I've endured a lot in my life, but that hurt worse than anything I've ever experienced.

I know they will follow me, so I turn down a few back roads to lose anyone who tries to follow. I just need some time to myself before I go back. I will go back because love is worth fighting for. I know he acted out of fear over everything that's been happening , but that still doesn't make it right. He needs to trust me completely also before I can continue in this relationship. I deserve it, and I won't settle for anything less.

I drive for about an hour then pull over to a gas station to get gas, and that's when

I realize I don't have my purse.

"Shit." I don't have anything. No money, no cell phone, no phone numbers. I lean my head back onto the head rest, and take a deep breath.

I walk inside and go to the counter for help. "Excuse me, is there anyway you can Google the phone number to Francine's Diner and Hotel and call them for me?"

The young lady behind the counter is very helpful, and hands me her cell phone when the call goes through.

"Francine's Diner and Hotel, how may I help you?" Grandpa answers, and its so good to hear his voice.

"John, its Carrie."

"Carrie, how are you honey? My grandson giving you trouble girl?" He laughs sweetly.

"I need you to call Chance, and tell him to come and get me." I sniffle.

"Where are you?" The concern in his voice is an emotional pull on my heart.

"I'm okay I just need a ride." I give him the address, and my promise that I will be safe.

"I love you my girl." Grandpa hangs up before I can reply.

I sit in my truck feeling exhausted, and emotionally drained.

I must have dozed off because Chance's face is at my window tapping to get my attention. He has a black eye, and a busted lip. I unlock the door then scoot over.

"Move over, please." Chance starts up my truck, and then pulls to the pumps to fill my tank, and gets me a coffee to go.

When he gets back behind the wheel I notice Sonny wave as he drives off on Chance's motorcycle.

I don't say anything, and neither does he. The ride back is strained from the silence.

I watch the scenery go by until I can't take it anymore. "Chance.....I...."

"Shut up, please." He grits out as his hands strain on the steering wheel tight. He takes a few deep breaths then pulls off onto a deserted side road, and turns the truck off.

My eyes are watering, and I can feel myself choking on my emotions. I try to swallow.

He turns to me, unfastens my seat belt, then pulls me into his arms. He is squeezing me tightly constricting my breathing, but I don't care.

"I'm so sorry." I can feel his hot breath on my neck. "I know that you didn't do anything wrong." He pulls a breath to try and stop the little sob from escaping him, but I hear it. "I was so fucking jealous when I saw those photos. You were happy, and safe with Sonny. It wasn't me you were looking at. When you left I thought you were leaving me. You had every right to leave, but when you called for me not Justine, or anyone else, to come and get you I realized you weren't leaving me. We had a fight, and I was an asshole. I begged for Sonny's forgiveness, and now I need yours. I'm so sorry baby." He leans back, and cups my cheek where I see his tears.

"Yes, I forgive you. I wasn't leaving you. I just needed some time to myself to get my emotions under control. Sonny is my friend, and you need to except that. I won't be told who I allow into my life ever again." I wipe his eyes. "It looks like Sonny got you good." I kiss his eye, and lip.

"Oh, this isn't from Sonny. This is from Justine." I laugh, as he laughs. "Ow, ow, ow.... Don't make me laugh." He pulls me to him.

"I spent all my marriage to Alex doing what he wanted, acting how he wanted, and being someone that wasn't me. I laid down, and literally took whatever he felt was his right to take even though I already said no. I will never be that woman again for anyone. I'm stronger, and more independent than I have ever been."

"I fell in love with the strong independent woman before me. I don't want you any other way. We're going to disagree, fight, and be down right dumb sometimes, but I need you to stick around, and knock me on my ass if that's what it takes. I just can't handle you leaving."

"Well, the dumb part falls on you. In all those photos of Sonny, and I do you know what put that happy, and safe look on my face?"

"Tell me."

"You, you dummy. We were talking about love, and trust. His feelings for Emily, and my feelings for you. He told me about his injury before he came home. He was trying to help me understand that you love me,and my heart even if I can't give you babies. He loves Emily, and trusts her enough to give her his whole heart to take care of even though he can't give her babies. I need to let that worry go, and know that I'm enough too."

"Who knew he was so wise." Chance takes my mouth softly. Kissing, and nibbling on my lips then down my neck.

"I'll tell him you think so."

"Wench" He bites me harder.

"Take me home, and spank your wench." I nip his shoulder.

"I can't your daughter arrived before I left, and she was pissed. I thought I was going to have two black eyes."

I start laughing hard.

"You think that's funny, huh?" He scoots to the middle of the seat, and puts me straddling his lap where my skirt rises up to my panties. "Damn, that's hot." He traces his finger across my white panties.

"Spank me." I kneel up onto my knees, as his left hand pushes his middle finger inside my panties.

"You've been a bad girl Carrie." His right hand cracks my ass cheek.

"Yes, I have. Now, punish me." I cry out as he pushes two fingers inside.

I gush as his palm makes contact with my ass again. "Fuck yes." I ride his fingers.

"Take my cock out, and ride me now Carrie." His palm connects with my bare ass after he rips my underwear aside.

I quickly take him out, and line him up. I take him all at once. I'm so fucking wet for him. I bounce up and down, as he pushes up into me hard over, and over. I reach down, and play with my clit. I lean back against the dash to give him a clear view of us connected.

"Baby, oh god, you're so fucking beautiful when your full of me."

"I'm coming Chance."

"Fuck yes!" He squeezes me tight down onto him, as he fills me up, and I spray all over him.

A truck goes by honking at us, and we quickly look up. We start laughing at ourselves, but we're still connected.

"I could live connected to you forever." I squeeze my internal muscles.

"Carrie." He moans, holding me to him.

"Can you grab some tissues out of the glove box?" I continue to suck on his neck as he leans to get the tissues. I lick and nip until he hands me some.

"Hold these." He pulls himself free and slowly begins to wipe me clean. He uses his fingers to spread me wide open.

"You're teasing." I moan.

"Tonight when we go to bed I plan on finishing what I wanted to do to you this morning." He flicks my clit one more time before he pulls my panties back in place then cleaning himself, and fastening his jeans.

"Ready?"

"Lets go see that amazing granddaughter of yours."

"Okay" I scoot over beside him, and hold his arm as his hand grabs my inner thigh.

We pull up, and everyone is outside.

"How much trouble am I in?" I laugh softly, but it makes me feel very loved seeing everyone outside waiting for me.

"With everything that's been happening lately everyone's nerves are more on edge. They all love you."

"Oh god, Nana and Grandpa." Two chairs are at the front of the group inside of the open garage. I jump out, and go straight to them for hugs.

"Chance says we're going to have a fancy meal." Nana whispers to me.

"Yes, we are." Now I feel even more guilty knowing I put Sonny behind on his cooking.

I hug everyone, and when I don't see Sonny, I look to Emily.

"He's at the diner finishing up preparation."

"Will you take me over?" I ask Chance.

"Sure, come on everyone. Please feel free to enjoy my home. We will be back to get everyone when its ready."

Chance walks me over after I promise Destiny I'll be right back to get her. She wants to help set the tables.

"He's in the kitchen." Chance starts to lead me back.

"I want to go back alone. I will bring him out in a minute okay?"

"Sure, I'll wait right here." Chance kisses me then sits down at the counter.

"Are you avoiding me Sonny?" I enter just as he is drying his hands.

"No, I just thought I would get caught up on things." He continues wiping his hands on the towel.

"Thanks for being my friend." I hesitate because he doesn't seem to want to look at me.

"I am your friend Carrie. I also know what its like to be so fucking jealous I do dumb shit like what Chance did. He loves you."

"I know he does, but I also know he won't interfere in my friendship with you again. I can't live that way ever again. We talked about all of it."

"So, you two are okay?"

"Yes, I love him, and he loves me."

"Good, you deserve it." He turns back to the sink.

"That's it? You have nothing else?" I walk up behind him.

"Nope." He turns around and crosses his arms across his chest.

"You men are dumb asses!" I say a little hurt. I walk back into the dining room.

"Hey! What the hell did I do?" Sonny follows me out.

I march right up to Chance, and get in his face. "Tell the dumb ass he can hug me." I demand feeling a little choked up.

"Easy tiger." Chance grabs me to calm me down.

"I was a fucking dumb ass Sonny. I will apologize again if it will help. You're my best friend, and I had no right to be jealous over those photos."

"Yes, you did." Sonny mumbles.

"No, I didn't. If it was anyone else maybe, but not you. You're my brother, and I know you wouldn't have crossed a line that would have hurt me. Now, get your ass over her, and hug her you big dumb ass." Chance slaps Sonny on the back when he comes over, and takes me from him.

Sonny picks me up off my feet. "If I wasn't so madly in love with his niece then I could give him a good run for his money doll face." He winks as I wipe my eyes.

"Shut up dork." I step back under Chance's arm feeling better.

Chance laughs as he pulls Sonny into our circle for a three way hug. Then we step apart to get this meal going.

"I need to go get Destiny. I promised she could help set the tables."

"I'll go get her, and you can stay to help Sonny." Chance looks over to Sonny. "Where is Henry?" He looks around.

"He went out back when Carrie came in. Taking the trash out for me."

"Okay." He leaves to go get Destiny.

"Why doesn't Henry ever come over like you do? He's more than welcome."

"I asked him once why he is always alone, and never comes out into the dining room area. He said he doesn't like people." Sonny laughs at my face. "Don't take it personally he has always been that way. I know he served in the Army. I only know that because of his tattoo on his arm. He's a nice enough guy he just doesn't talk much."

"Okay, well lets get started. We can have everything lined up on a long table, and everyone can serve themselves. That way we can all enjoy ourselves, including Henry."

"Good luck with that doll face."

"Oh don't worry, I have ammunition." I turn as Chance comes in with Destiny on his shoulders.

"Mamaw!" She scrambles down Chance's shoulders to get to me.

"There's my girl." I hug her to me.

"I want to help!" She is jumping up, and down.

"Lets get the plates, and silverware. Oh, and a stack of cups." We head into the kitchen to get started.

I make a few trips to get enough plates. Destiny grabs a handful each of forks, spoons.

"Maybe just a few more."

"Okay." She runs into the kitchen for more, as I put the napkin dispensers on the long table with the plates.

"Carrie." Chance grabs my hand.

"Huh? I need to go after Destiny." I start to follow her.

"She's fine. Henry's in there he will make sure she doesn't get hurt. Come here." He pulls me up against him.

"What are you doing?" I laugh when he starts kissing my neck. "We have to get everything ready."

"Hey, knock that off, and help me with these extra chairs." Sonny comes up from the storage room in the cellar.

"Anybody ever tell you that your timing sucks." Chance smacks my ass as he goes to help Sonny.

I hear Sonny laughing when I head for the kitchen.

That back door opens, and Henry comes in at the same time as I do.

"Destiny!" She is standing up on a shelf trying to reach something.

Henry quickly grabs her, and helps her down. He looks down at us, as I hug her to me.

He pulls down a container that says cookies.

"I just wanted a cookie."

"You can't climb on everything monkey."

Henry hands her a cookie then turns, and goes back to work, but not before I see him smirk.

"I like to climb. Daddy says he's going to build me a tree house, but mommy says she's already getting gray's.

"A tree house huh?"

"What are gray's?"

"Something mommy's get in our hair from our kids being monkeys." I tweak her nose causing her to giggle.

"I love you Mamaw." She throws her arms around me.

"You make my heart beat baby girl." I squeeze her to me for a second before she runs off into the dining room.

I stand up staring after her smiling.

"She's a handful." Henry quietly says.

I try to hide the surprise from my face that he talked to me."Yes, she is. She gives me another gray every time I see her."

He turns back around chuckling.

I head back into the dining room where there is music softly playing, and Chance is twirling Destiny around.

"Everything good?" I ask Sonny while watching Destiny laugh.

"Yeah, every things ready. We just need to fill the table, and get the guests.

"It smells mouthwatering, and delicious in that kitchen."

"Thank you." Sonny beams with pride.

"Your Gamma is smiling down on you." I pull his cheek down to me, and kiss him then go dance with my man, and sweet granddaughter.

"Hey beautiful." Chance pulls me into his arms, and the three of us dance around for a minute.

"Sonny says everything is ready we just need the guest."

"Is that a hint to hurry up?"

"Yes, now hurry up I'm starving, and the smells from that kitchen are calling my name."

"Okay." He kisses me then takes off.

"I can help!" Destiny takes off after Chance.

I step outside just as she grabs his hand.

"I got her." Chance throws her up onto his shoulders and heads to the house.

I get Henry, and Sonny to help me get all the food on the table.

"You out did yourself Sonny. This looks amazing."

"Thanks doll face." He winks at me just as Chance comes in with all the guest in tow except Greg.

We're all sitting around eating, laughing, and talking when the kitchen door swings open. Its Crystal, and Henry is behind her.

"This is not the time." Henry says to her.

"Crystal we can take this outside. There is no reason to interrupt everyone's meal." Chance stands up to intervene.

"Oh, I didn't come here to see you Chance. I came here to see Connie." She looks right at me.

"Its Carrie, and all three of us can step outside." I stand up. "Everyone please continue your meal."

I grab Chance's hand, and we follow Crystal back out through the kitchen into the alley. Crystal looks like she has been crying.

"Spit it out." Chance says kind of rude and she flinches.

"I came to apologize." She lowers her head.

"Apologize! After everything you have done do you really believe that will be enough?" Chance looks disgusted.

"I started my period yesterday in the Doctors office. I thought for sure I was pregnant, but before she could do a test I started bleeding. She said my stress lately was what caused my period to be late for three months."

"Stress over what?" I ask.

"My business is failing, and the only way I could get Chance to my bed was to get him drunk. I knew you couldn't stand me." She wipes her eyes and turns around.

"What about the positive pregnancy test taped to the bag?" He asks.

"I paid a pregnant woman to take the test for me."

"You're such a bitch Crystal." Chance runs his hands through his hair in agitation. "The photos of me from my past with other women was stupid, but breaking into my house!"

"I only wanted to scare her off. I never really did crawl into your bed. I'm sorry!" Her shoulders are shaking, and she is sobbing when she turns around.

"What about poisoning her coffee, and taking a naked photo of her in the shower! Huh?" Chance grabs her face, and jerks it up.

"Chance." I grab his arm.

"No! She hurt you dammit!"

"I never touched her coffee. I wouldn't poison anybody, and I sure as hell didn't photograph her in the shower. I'm not into women asshole!" She jerks back, and wipes her face.

"I swear to fucking god Crystal I'll have you locked up!"

"I didn't do it Chance. I just wanted to make her jealous, and get her to leave. I love you."

"Get the fuck out of my sight!" Chance yells at her, and she turns and runs.

"Hey." I turn his face to me. "I'm okay." I wrap my arms around him.

"Keeping you safe is all that matters to me."

"I'm okay." I put my lips to his. "I'm okay." I feel so much relief that she isn't pregnant with his child. "Are you disappointed even a little that your not going to be a daddy? Its okay to be disappointed." I stare into his eyes.

"If I would have been a daddy I would have loved that child with every breath in my body. I'm a protector Carrie, and I would have protected your heart, and made damn sure you were by my side every second. Loving a child wouldn't have made me love you any less."

"I would have stood by your side even if she would have been pregnant with your child."

"I know."

"I'm sorry, but I'm happy that shes not." I whisper against his lips.

"I know that too." He takes my mouth and devours my lips. The deepness of his kiss is hot, and possessive.

A throat clears. "Boss."

"Go away Henry." Chance bites my neck, and licks me to soothe the sting.

I hear him chuckle as the door closes.

Chance puts my back to the door. "Your mine." I hear his zipper.

"Your mine." I raise my skirt, and then wrap my legs around his waist.

He shoves my panties aside, and pushes up inside of me.

"I'm home." He buries his face into my neck.

We step back inside of the kitchen hand in hand.

"Everything okay?" Justine rushes in.

"Yes, its okay." I smile, and hug my friend.

"That damn Henry wouldn't let us in the kitchen." Justine glares at Henry who is smiling.

"Thanks Henry."

"No problem sweetheart." He winks at me.

"Hey! What the hell is wrong with all you men? Stop flirting with my woman." Chance hits Henry with a dish towel.

"Can't help myself Boss." His face is serious until he turns around, and smirks at Sonny who is standing behind Justine.

"Knock it off Sonny." I laugh at Chance's growling. "He's learned his lesson."

"Woman!"

"Excuse me I'm starving." I hurry up, and get out of the kitchen while Sonny, and Henry laugh their asses off.

By the time we get back to Chance's its after eight, and Greg has nothing to report.

"I'm sorry you missed out, but we brought left overs for you to enjoy." Emily sits down the platter.

"You ready to head out Em?" Sonny takes her hand.

Greg and Justine head over to the hotel behind Sonny and Emily.

"You have the guest room off the kitchen tonight Alexa. Destiny can have the couch if she wants."

"Yea! A fort, I want a fort!"

"First, how about we pick out a movie then we can make a fort, have some popcorn, and enjoy the movie."

"Chance can do it. Please!" Destiny jumps up and down with excitement.

"Okay, Chance it is." I hug her.

"I want to watch Black Beauty." Destiny pulls Chance to the movies.

"I don't have that movie, but I do have Racing Stripes from when Em was younger."

"What's that?"

"Its about horses, but the main character is a racing donkey who doesn't know he's not a horse."

"Wow, a real donkey? Okay, lets watch that one."

Alexa pulls me into the kitchen while Chance helps Destiny with the movie.

"You can grab extra blanket from the hall closet Nick." I nod to the hall.

"Sit down mom." Alexa pulls me to a chair.

"Whats going on?"

She grabs my hand and lays it on her stomach. "I'm five months."

I know she hinted at it but I didn't realize she was that far along. I now notice the much baggier clothes, and the belly bulge.

"I knew from the look you gave me at your house, but my god, oh Alexa." I cry happy tears.

"We had a few complications, and I wanted to be sure before I gave you details. I was scared."

"I'm your mom baby, you can tell me anything. I'm here through good, and bad." I bite my lip to stop the trembling. "I would have been there."

"I know, but you've had a lot on your mind. Nick, and I decided to keep this for ourselves for awhile. I love you so much mom. Please don't be hurt."

"I just want the best for you baby girl. I'm so happy to be a Mamaw again." I hug her to me.

"I need to tell dad yet. I couldn't tell him last week, not until I told you. I figured I'd just wait till we got here."

"I'm sure he will be happy for you." I keep my tone neutral.

"I know you don't like talking about him much. I do have certain memories from my childhood mom."

"What memories?" I sit up straight, and concerned.

"I know he wasn't always a nice man."

"You know he loves you."

"I wasn't talking about me." She grabs my hand.

"Alexa."

"Mom, you are such a strong woman now. I've seen the changes, and I'm so proud of you."

"Thank you. You are the best gift your dad ever gave me. For that I will always be grateful."

"You're a great mom, a great Mamaw, and according to Chance, a great girlfriend." She wiggles her eyebrows.

"He is a pretty great boyfriend." I turn and watch the guys build Destiny a fort to settle in for the movie.

"Mamaw, can we have popcorn now please?" Destiny comes running into the kitchen.

"Sure, baby girl." I laugh at her whirlwind energy, as she runs back to the living room. "Duty calls."

I make some popcorn, and we all settle in for the movie.

Chance

Life goes back to everyday things. I work the diner, Carrie writes while helping with Nana, or in the diner once in awhile, and Sonny continues to be with Em.

Tomorrow we are heading to Tennessee to watch Destiny in her Junior racing competition. Carrie is excited to see her. Its been over three weeks, and I'm looking forward to it also.That little girl wormed her way right into my heart.

I walk into the kitchen where Carrie is staring hard into the back yard lost in thought.

"Hey beautiful." I pull her braid to the side so I can suck on her soft neck. Her sweetness is addictive. "Whats on your mind?"

"Don't you find it odd that nothing has happened in weeks. I mean I'm happy about it, but I feel edgy also. Like something bad is coming."

"I won't let anything happen to you." I pull a necklace out of my pocket, and put it around her neck. "My phone number is on the back, and anytime you need me just open the locket, and I'll come for you. No matter where or when. You have to promise me you will wear this at all times until we catch whoever is doing this. I'm feeling paranoid myself."

"Its beautiful. I promise I'll wear it everyday." She turns around and kisses me.

"Someday you are going to be my wife." I lick her neck.

"Chance" She stiffens and turns back around.

"Don't fret baby, I said someday." I bite her, and leave my mark on her.

She relaxes back into me, and puts her arms up and around the back of my neck while wiggling her ass against me.

"You want something?" I kiss her neck.

"Maybe"

"Ask me." I use my hands to slowly pull her skirt up from behind.

"Touch me." She moans.

I run my fingers up until I snag the band on her panties, and push them down her thighs.

She wiggles till they fall to the floor where she kicks them off.

"Is that enough?" I tease her by cupping her breasts.

"I want more."

I unhook her bra then pull her shirt over her head while her bra slides down her arms.

"How much more? Tell me." I skim my palms lightly over her nipple. They are hard peaks.

"Pinch my nipples. Oh yeah, harder please."

I roll her nipples then stretch them out until she moans in pleasure.

She turns around, and grabs my hands to put them back on her breasts, and squeezes them together. "Bite me."

I back her up to the table, and lift her up onto it. "Lose the skirt." I push her backwards.

She arches her hips up to push her skirt down, and off. She is sprawled out before me like a feast on the table.

I lean down and suck her nipple into my mouth, scraping my teeth gently across her causing her nipple to get harder, and redden even more. I continue between both breast until she is squirming uncontrollably.

"Are you wet for me?" I slide my hand up her inner thigh until I reach her slit. She is already dripping down her lips onto her ass, and the table.

"Are you hungry?" She pulls her legs up, and out to display herself wide open for me.

"I'm starving." I lean down, and run my tongue up her slit scooping up her juices. "Delicious and mine." I dive back in holding her legs wide open to eat her out until she screams with her orgasm.

"Come here." She pulls my hair hard.

"I'm not done." I bite her inner thigh then push two fingers up inside of her.

"Oh fuck!" She flops back onto the table not letting go of my hair.

"Put your hands out and grab the edges of the table." I pry her fingers from my scalp. "Now Carrie."

I shove my fingers back inside of her while she does as I want. "Good girl." I curl my fingers to bring her pleasure to a peak, and slowly push my thumb against her asshole when I suck her clit hard into my mouth.

"Chance! Please now. Please!" She cries and pulls at my hair when her next orgasm hits my tongue like a waterfall.

"Please what?" I tower above her limp body. Her legs are dangling across my forearms still wide open.

"Fuck me." She moans.

"Beg me." I push my painfully hard cock just inside of her while she tries to lift her hips to push me in further.

"Please fuck me dammit!" Growling, she pulls my hair hard.

"God damn that's hot." I slam into her over and over until I can't move the table anymore. I swell up so hard and explode all inside of her walls, and she is screaming my name until she is hoarse.

I lean my weight onto her trying to catch my breath.

"I think you broke the table." She pants into my ear.

"So worth it." I chuckle when I pick myself up off her. "Give me a minute, and I will help you up."

"I think I'll stay right here because I can't move."

She is sprawled wide open with her legs dangling off the table with my beard scratches all over her breast, and my cum dripping down her ass crack. She is plump, and ripe looking. More beautiful, and satisfied looking than I've ever seen her.

I grab a warm washcloth, and clean her up before we head upstairs.

We get up early to head for Tennessee. Sonny said he would keep an eye on the house, and help Emily with Nana and Grandpa. Henry is going to help with my shifts at the diner while were gone for the weekend to spend time with Alexa, and see Destiny's competition.

We decided to ride my Harley. Its starting to get colder so I figure one more ride for the soul. We dress warm and hit the road.

We stop once for coffee just to warm up a little then arrive at Alexa's around eleven a.m.

"You should let me ride that badass bike." Nick is practically drooling over my ride.

"Sorry man, but nobody sits on my bike, but me, and my lady behind me." I laugh as he pouts all the way into the house.

"Chance!" Destiny throws herself at me.

"Hi Sunshine." I fling her up onto my shoulders.

"What am I chopped liver?" Carrie pulls on one of Destiny's braids so she'll lean down for a kiss.

"I've been training so hard Mamaw. I just know I'm going to win." She can't hold still as she bounces all over my shoulders.

"Well, no matter what place you get you're already a winner."

"Lunch will be ready soon then we need to head out. It starts at one o'clock." Alexa sets some plates around the table.

"Aw, mom. I can't eat I need to go sit with bubblegum." Destiny whines.

"You're just going to have to suffer through it young lady."

"Yes Ma'am." She slides down off my shoulders to sit at the table, as if its the end of the world.

"I made your favorite." Alexa sets down a big bowl of macaroni and cheese then hot dogs.

Thirty minutes later we're on our way to the competition in Nick's big truck, and trailer that has Bubblegum in it.

The crowd is a lot bigger than I thought. There is at least a thousand people in the stands.

We sit through quite a few riders before Destiny comes out. She is sitting tall and proud. The course is easily ran by Bubblegum, and I think Carrie may need more tissues then she has in her hands.

"She scored high. Yes! Look at her, she is so awesome. Aw, my baby girl."

I pull her to me. "Proud Mamaw?"

"Very."

We watch the last few riders, and she places second.

"Did you see me?" She is in the barn brushing down Bubblegum.

"We sure did Sunshine." I grab her up onto my shoulders.

"I only got second place."

"Hey, second place is a hard earned placed. You should be proud of yourself because I know I am Sunshine."

"Thanks Chance." I feel her kiss the top of my head, as her hands hold onto my chin.

"Come on baby girl lets get Bubblegum loaded up into the trailer." Nick grabs Destiny off my shoulders.

"Need some help?"

"You can back the trailer up to that end of the barn if ya like."

"Sure man." I run ahead to help out.

"Keys are in it." Nick hollers as he grabs Bubblegum's reigns.

I get in the truck. Its a nice truck, fully loaded with all the stops and whistles as my Grandpa use to say.

Having a little time away from the diner to enjoy my Harley, my woman, and her family feels real good.

Mississippi will always be my home, but Tennessee is gorgeous. The views are breathtaking.

I told Carrie we will try to come here at least once every two weeks. I know she misses her daughter, and that little Sunshine granddaughter of hers is a great kid.

Carrie said Nick is really a hard working, honest man, and I can really see that in him. He seems like a great father too.

I get out and help Nick lower the ramps to walk Bubblegum up.

"I still don't see why I can't stay back here with her. What if she gets scared? She may need me daddy."

"Squirt, you know its not safe. Now stop whining, and get the door."

"Okay daddy."

I have to hide my smirk when she hangs her head with her bottom lip out.

"We're all set. Lets get your mom, and Mamaw."

I throw Destiny up on my shoulders, and take off galloping like a horse, and trying my best to sound like Bubblegum.

"You're silly Chance." She giggles as she bounces around everywhere. "You sound more like the donkey on Racing Stripes."

"A donkey! You little runt, just for that I'm breaking out the tickle monster." I bring her down to my arms and start tickling her till she screams in mercy for me to stop.

"I have to pee!"

I instantly stop. "Whoa, no more tickling. She's all yours mom." I send her to her moms side. "Where's Carrie?" I just realized she isn't here.

"She went over to the restrooms then she was going to bring something special back for Destiny. She shouldn't be long."

"Okay." I look around at the crowd beginning to clear out, and I just don't feel right about her not being in my sight. I'm going to go see if she needs any help." I feel like I mutter the last part as I head toward the restrooms.

The line is long, and I start searching, but I still don't see her. I wait a few moments and four other women have come out, but not Carrie.

"Excuse me." I stop the next woman at the front of the line. "Can you see if there is a woman named Carrie in there? I'd really appreciate it."

"Sure handsome." The lady winks at me.

I wait a minute for her to come back out.

"Sorry honey, but no Carrie."

"Thanks anyway." I head toward the concession stand.

I'm trying to see through the crowd. People are everywhere trying to get food, and groups are standing around talking, and even though its thinned out it still seems packed.

"Carrie!" I begin to holler. "Carrie!" People are beginning to look at me. The more time that goes by and I can't find her, the more I'm panicking.

"Carrie!"

"Hey, you didn't find her yet?" Nick pulls me around.

"No, and she's not in the restroom either. Where is the announcers box so I can page her?"

"Back here."

We go and have her name called, but its not enough.

"Fuck!" I pace back, and forth. "She wouldn't have just left, she.... Wait, wait, wait! I put a tracker in her necklace. Shit, I can't believe I forgot." I pull out my cell phone, and it shows she is moving, but its miles away from here.

"You put a tracker on her?" Nick sees the map on my phone.

"She knows about it. Call me a paranoid fucker, but I don't care. I need a car dammit!" I'm running toward the parking lot. "Call the cops, and tell them what is going on."

"Wait, wait a minute Chance. Hold on, I can get you wheels." Nick pulls out his cell. "Come on."

I follow him back to the barns where a few guys are still standing around. Nick runs up to a guy and within seconds throws me a set of keys to a pick up.

"Drive!" He jumps into the passenger seat, and I'm on the move before my door shuts.

"Here, tell me where to go." I throw my phone at him so I can concentrate on the road.

"Who knew she would be here?" Nick asks.

"Just our friends, but let me ask you something. When is the last time you've seen Alex?" I know its that fucker. I can feel it in my gut.

"He came to see Destiny awhile ago. He was here the day before Carrie called about being sick in the hospital. He's been talking to Destiny on the phone a lot more lately. Do you really think he is the one who's been fucking with Carrie?"

"How much do you know about what went on in their relationship?" I can feel my knuckles hurting from gripping the steering wheel so tight.

"Not a lot. I know a lot wasn't good. Carrie hates talking about him. She always seemed vulnerable I guess is the word. I can tell you that I never really liked the asshole. He always bothered me for some reason. Here, turn up here. We're catching up, its just about another mile."

"I'll kill the motherfucker...."

"You just worry about getting Carrie, and let me get his ass."

We come up on a dark blue car that won't pull over, so I cut in front of him, and slam on my brakes.

I'm out of the truck and ripping the drivers door open. Its Crystal.

"Where is she!" I rip her out of the car and slam her over the hood. "Where is she ! You tell me or I'll break your fucking neck." I feel spit flying out of my mouth.

"She's not here!" Nick hollers from searching the car and the trunk.

"I don't know what you're talking about, please! You're hurting me." Crystal cries.

I look down, and she is wearing Carrie's necklace. I rip it off, and shove it in her face. "Where did you get this?" I demand.

"You're fucking crazy Chance! My boyfriend just gave it to me. Whats wrong with you?"

"We're you at the riding competition?" Nick asks.

"Yes, my boyfriend said his granddaughter was riding in it. Her name is Destiny." She is blubbering.

"Where are you supposed to meet him?" Nick continues the questioning as I let her go before I really lose my shit.

"He said he would call me later. He gave me his car because he borrowed my truck. What the hell is going on?" She is crying uncontrollably now.

"This is Carrie's! That boyfriend of yours is her crazy ass ex husband. He took her!" I punch the hood, and pull my hair trying to think what to do. "Think damn you!" I try to grab her, but Nick holds me off.

"Chance"

"He.... He said he had a cabin that he is renting. He said the winery down the road was the best tasting wine around." She is still crying. "I'm sorry, I'm trying!"

I know I must seem like a scary motherfucker right now.

"Alexa, yeah, yeah, slow down baby. Listen okay, do you know of any log cabin rentals in the area that has a winery near by? I know, please baby just think." Nick has his back to us as he talks to Alexa.

"Mountain Ash Cabin Rentals, got it. Yes, I know. I love you too. Hang on babe, I promise we'll get her back." He hangs up the phone.

"Come on, Alexa found the name of the place. You drive and I'll GPS it."

"You take this car straight to the authorities tell them everything, and to get to Mountain Ash Cabin Rentals. Go now Crystal!"

Twenty five minutes later in the opposite direction we finally get to the cabins. There is six of them, but only one has Crystal's truck in the driveway.

"I'm going around the back. You see if any windows are open or something. Just give me two minutes to find her before we alert him that we're here."

I ease into the back door, and I can hear him talking, but I can't make out the words. I go in a little closer until I hear a click at the back of my head.

"You just don't learn do you boy toy?" Alex pushes the barrel into my head to push me forward.

He forces me into a room where a big man is bent over, but I can't see his face. I do see Carrie's boots in front of him.

"Ow! You fucking bitch." He backhands her after she headbutts him.

I feel my stomach drop at the sound of his voice, and I realize who it is. I charge at him. "You bastard!" I stop short when he grabs her by the throat, and puts her in front of him.

"Well, well, well, maybe this night will turn out better after all." He wipes blood off his nose.

"How could you fucking betray me like this Henry? I trusted you with my family." I seethe.

"Poor Chance you never have enough do you? The perfect family, the diner, this beauty." He licks up the side of her face. "You shouldn't have fucked my girl

Chance."

"What the fuck are you talking about?" I can't stop looking at how scared Carrie is.

"Crystal was mine!"

"What! Crystal has been in a lot of beds man. How the hell would I have known she was yours?"

"It doesn't matter now because I'm going to let you see how it feels to see me fuck her like I saw your drunk ass fuck Crystal." He squeezes her breast, and she screams through her gag.

"Stop it!" I charge him, and I don't care if I get shot in the back or not. I can't let him hurt her.

I'm in a haze beating Henry's face over, and over as the noise in the background fades. I hear her crying for me to stop.

"Please Chance, stop or you'll kill him. I need you baby."

I turn to her, and her gag has been pulled down, but her wrists are still tied with blood on them.

I steps into her space, and I drop to my knees to bury my face into her lap. I wrap my arms around her, and squeeze her to me. I need to feel her against me.

Nick has Alex on the floor sitting on him while he screams like a banshee.

"Carrie." I choke on my breath. I untie her bloody wrists, and pull her in my arms.

The police rush in, and everything is chaos for the next hour.

We're setting in the emergency room answering all kinds of questions on what happened when the nurses come rushing the room next to us with a code blue being hollered loudly.

"That's Alex in the room next to us. Nick shot him to save me." Carrie holds onto me.

"I owe Nick everything."

"He would have killed me. I can't believe he hated me that much."

"I don't think he hated you. I think he decided you were worth money, and he could get away with it for insurance money. He has something wrong with his mind, and you can't take that personally. He's fucked up. The Detective said he found evidence where he was going to make it look like you killed yourself. Don't you shed one fucking tear for that bastard. The only good thing he ever did for you was give you Alexa."

"That doesn't make any sense. If he wanted it to look like a suicide then why would he poison my coffee?"

"The coffee was actually meant for me. Henry did that, and he is the one who took a picture of you in the shower."

"I'm sorry about your friend."

"Some friend." I can't believe I cared about him. I didn't have a clue that he was trying to hurt us.

"He was your friend honey."

"Yeah, who wanted to hurt you!"

"Stop it, you couldn't have known, and I'm safe. Thanks to you, and Nick." She rubs my arm.

"I can't get that image of you out of my mind." I bury my face into her neck.

"I love you."

"I love you too baby."

We stay close, and just hold each other until we hear a nurse call the time of death.

"Oh god, I need to tell Alexa."

I pull back to touch the bandages on her wrists, and the bruises on her arms. "You do what you need to baby....."

"What?"

"I'm not sorry he is dead." I mean that with every breath I take.

"I know. Now, can you please see if we can get out of here?"

"Okay." I find a nurse, and she says as soon as the paperwork is ready we're free to go. In the mean time they need Carrie's bed, so we wait in the family waiting room.

Carrie walks up to her daughter, and they cry together. I see her quietly tell her about her father, and Alexa begins to cry even harder. I know its taring Carrie up when she has to tell her who kidnapped her. We head back to Alexa's house.

Alexa is grief stricken, and extremely angry, but thank god she has Nick. He is comforting her while Destiny sleeps on the couch.

Carrie sits on my lap. "I need to call Sonny, and check in."

"Babe, he's got it. He just told you an hour ago he has it under control. Come on, lets go to bed." We crawl in bed, and cuddle together.

"I love you so damn much." I breathe her scent into my lungs while I hold her tight to me. I fall asleep right where I want to be.

We spend two extra days to help Alexa get through the funeral before we head home to Mississippi.

Carrie

We've been going to Tennessee every weekend for the last three weeks because Alexa was due a couple of days ago. She has been admitted into the hospital to be induced, but she went into labor before we arrived.

We're setting in the waiting room with Destiny waiting to hear the news when Nick comes out smiling from ear to ear.

"Would you all like to come meet my son?"

We all rush to him for hugs, and congratulations then he leads us back.

Alexa is holding my grandson looking exhausted, and happy. She offers the baby to me.

"Oh my god, he is so tiny." Chance extends his finger, and the baby latches on.

"Hold out your arms." I put the baby into his arms.

"Chance, I want you to meet Lucas Chance Knight." Nick tells him.

"Really?" He is mesmerized by Lucas. His voice is so soft, as if he is afraid to be too loud. "I'm speechless." His voice catches.

"You're the best thing that's happened to my mom in a long time, and I wanted you to know how much we love you for it." Alexa has tears in her eyes.

"Thank you." He squeezes my hand to pull me closer. He looks to Alexa. "Your mother means the world to me."

"I know, and that's why we want you to be Lucas, and Destiny's Godfather. You're an honorable, and protective man Chance."

Chance leans down, and kisses Lucas then looks at Destiny. "What do you say Sunshine, should I be your Godfather?" He is holding the blanket back for Destiny to see Lucas.

"Yes!" She jumps up and down.

"Okay, I except, but first I need to get my gift." He carefully hands Lucas back to his mommy.

He grabs a small gift box out of his pocket before he kneels at my feet.

"What are you doing?" I feel my heart beating out of my chest.

"Carrie, I want you to be my wife. You've invited me into your family, and showed me what it means to love you. I love the strong woman that you are. Will you do me the honor of loving me for the rest of our lives, and be my wife?"

I look up, and everyone is holding signs that say yes.

"Babe, please put my mind at ease. Will you marry me?" He slides a simple gold band with a diamond onto my finger.

"Yes!" I slide onto his lap, as he falls backwards onto his butt.

"Thank god."

"Welcome to the family Chance." Destiny jumps onto us both.

I'm so happy that I trusted my heart to Chance.

The End